SECRETS OF AN AGELESS JOURNEY

SECRETS OF AN AGELESS JOURNEY

"The Mysterious Gift"

MATTHEW SAGE

Illustrations and Images
C.R. Redcorn

authorHOUSE®

AuthorHouse™
1663 Liberty Drive
Bloomington, IN 47403
www.authorhouse.com
Phone: 1-800-839-8640

First published by AuthorHouse   10/28/2009

ISBN: 978-1-4490-4286-8 (e)
ISBN: 978-1-4490-4285-1 (sc)
ISBN: 978-1-4490-4284-4 (hc)

Library of Congress Control Number: 2009911496

Printed in the United States of America
Bloomington, Indiana

This book is printed on acid-free paper.

In memory of Madeline—my wife, companion, and friend on a wonderful journey together. This book would not have been possible without her inspiration, charisma, vivacity, and unique manner of encouragement. She will forever be the consciousness guiding my thoughts and aspirations.

ACKNOWLEDGEMENTS

It is somewhat challenging and overwhelming when it comes to acknowledging those that have given their support and encouragement in the writing of this book. What has been most rewarding is their sincere interest and welcoming friendship. Thank you, everyone.

Foremost, C. R. Redcorn and Kathryn Redcorn: I have immense gratitude and appreciation for their support and friendship. The book is greatly enhanced by the illustrations contributed by C. R. Redcorn, and the knowledge and insight of Kathryn Redcorn increased considerably the relevance of the book.

It would be a great disservice to the works of Francis La Flesche and Garrick A. Bailey not to mention the information and inspiration I have gained from their writings.

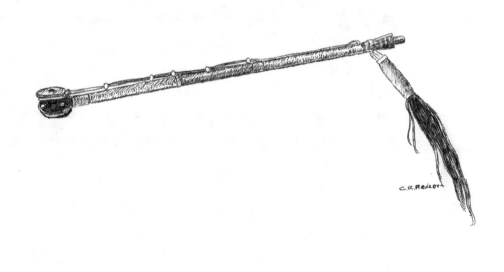

TABLE OF CONTENTS

PREFACE

This book began simply enough: after retiring on a small acreage in southeast Kansas, raising livestock soon became more of a hobby than a business. Our livestock and the mischievous wildlife must have missed the part about how they should interact with us. The old saying "what goes around comes around" is a more accurate description of their way of behaving. I began to write down their unusual, humorous, and sometimes spontaneous conduct in short stories.

The most remarkable of all the animals was a very clever and resourceful border collie acquired to help manage the cattle. It did not take long to appreciate the cattle dog's no-nonsense approach to sorting out all the problems, real or mysterious, and to putting all the inhabitants in their place. It became apparent his inborn mystique was not derived from the everyday world with which I was familiar.

I came to the conclusion that if he could easily exist in my everyday world so could I in his instinctive world of nature and spirit. In the pursuit of such an undertaking I found it impossible to keep a purely subjective perspective.

With Native American Indian culture as the only realistic and reliable authority on the subject, I began to make my way into the cattle dog's persona. Who knows how or why a challenge was eagerly accepted by the cattle dog and a rivalry came into being? It was a struggle just to stay one step ahead of the other: the cattle dog with his speed and cunning me with my human skills.

I am sure that it was a look of delight that came over him when he had done one better on me. Do not misunderstand—the cattle dog knew his responsibilities very well, responding to all my commands if they applied to the job at hand.

To my surprise other animals joined in the rivalry, mostly on my side, maybe just as payback for the cattle dog's manipulation or maybe just to make it fair. What became clear was that most of the animals understood humans much more than I had ever anticipated. In that unguarded and natural environment the animals took on individual personality traits that were in some ways similar to those of humans. "I really do have a life too, you know."

I could only imagine that some process of invading the border collie's domain had brought on this situation. To the cattle dog and the other animals, it must have been in some way a signal for a new order of the land—something like a new playing field. For some, they were stronger, faster, and more cunning, and I respected that. For others, domesticated or wild, I was a source of refuge and support, even to lodge complaints.

I knew I had gone too far when I began relating personality traits of an animal to an individual person, even though the philosophical metaphors were amazingly accurate in predicting behavior.

Still, that was on my part— what about the animals? I could only rationalize the close interaction between me and the animals shaped something of an extended family circle; it was even conceivable the animal members of the family became conversant by inference, predicting, or possibly as a result of some degree of theorizing. It did occur to me that possibly some controlling invisible force, maybe even a spiritual presence, was involved. What else?

In any case, it was not difficult to understand why in Native American Indian legends and traditions animals and humans are portrayed as relatives in a single, unified, and highly integrated system with all aspects of daily life having spiritual meaning and purpose.

What would it have been like to live in an age when Native American Indians viewed themselves as being one with the energies of the earth, nature, and all of the Great Spirit's creations? From my experience, participating in the natural order of life with our animals, I had very little knowledge and some basic skills when compared with the strength, slyness, and, yes, sneakiness of the animals.

It is no wonder Native American Indian legends tell of gifted ones who existed in both the visible, everyday world and in an invisible, spiritual world; something like a sixth sense where they became more perceptive to the subtle nature and inner meaning that exist around them. In time the idea of gifted ones became more compelling if thought of as having the presence within the community that secured balance and harmony.

Imaginary or not, I began to write about animals and birds, coexisting with humans each with their own individual intellects, a unique particular knowledge of the universe, and their own skillfulness for living in it. My once leisure activity with the animals turned into a quest for any fragment of information on the subject.

After a time the historical epic of one Native American Indian nation became the spirit of a book, *Secrets of an Ageless Journey: The Mysterious Gift*.

Many years have passed since a boy thirteen years old fashioned a halter and Indian blanket saddle based on a photograph of his number-one Indian warrior. The memory of that time, once replaced by worldly diversions and travel, can sometimes bring a tear. And that is how this book came about.

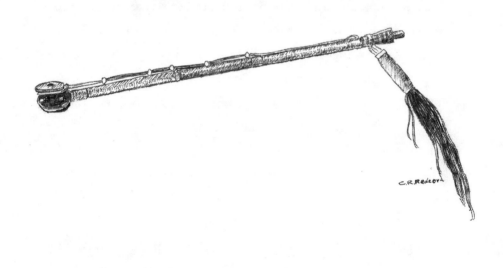

INTRODUCTION

Secrets of an Ageless Journey is a story bound portrayal of events in the lives of a Wazhazhe Indian family as they re-encounter their ancestral beliefs and a mystifying way of life, *The Mysterious Gift*—a fictional but plausible saga of a Wazhazhe Indian clan spanning seven generations.

An ancestral journal written in the early twentieth century influences the latest generation and mystifies one member as she ventures back into an earlier time when nature's purity, mysteries, and uniqueness guided their way of life.

To the Wazhazhe Indian Nation all life was the innovation of Wakonda, sometimes referred to as just the unknown or as the great, mysterious power. They believed that the Great Spirit's presence was everywhere and in all things, which included a corresponding invisible spiritual world that surrounded them.

Most of all they believed in a dynamic and ever-changing cosmos with everything in it having meaning and purpose, a state of balance in which they were not more important than the animals, birds, plants, or even inorganic material, although it was believed that humans did have the ability and responsibility to influence their destinies.

In their early days the Wazhazhe Indian Nation believed there were three divisions to their universe: the upper world, the lower world, and the middle world where they lived. They divided their villages into two separate communities, that of the Sky People and that of the Earth People. Their legends tell of the Sky People coming to earth to unite with the Earth People to form the Wazhazhe Nation—"The children of the middle water."

By all accounts, the Wazhazhe Nation developed a highly sophisticated and well-structured culture; rules and customs established by ancestral holy men, referred to as the men of mystery, influenced village life and their national policies.

To become one of the holy men, entrusted with the knowledge handed down by the men of mystery, training began during boyhood and continued for many years. To be accepted, a young boy had to undergo seven degrees of instruction, at each stage learning a progressively more complicated body of sacred knowledge.

Village life and harmony centered about the sacred fireplace and the supernatural world of Wakonda. The sacred fireplace in the middle of the religious leader's house represented the sun; a door opening to the east, the rising sun; and a door opening to the west, the setting sun; together they symbolized the uninterrupted flow of life.

Each family fireplace in the village was kindled from the religious leader's fireplace, uniting the families with a powerful sense of Wazhazhe identity. In their art, rituals, and customs was the humble reverence for the mysteries in nature and their creator. In that devoted culture there were those, gifted ones, who processed supernatural abilities, an extra sense or perception—not to be confused with a medicine man, witch doctor, or shaman that lived in the middle of the village and was involved in daily life.

As I ventured into the idea and the uniqueness of gifted ones, their supernatural abilities, and supernatural phenomena, it became clear the mystical perceptions were not as I first thought. It must be more like a Mysterious Gift, a mystifying shadowy influence, that of an awareness or realization of an invisible force, an inspiration, guiding one's existence.

The abilities of gifted ones were very much real as they devoted their lives with a spiritual reverence to the one who created the natural universe they sought. The path they followed was by choice to journey into nature's purest energies, where the spirits' world resides. For the Native Wazhazhe Indian Nation their energies became the bridge that unites man, animal, and the earth to the spirits. For some they very much exist today.

The Wazhazhe lived their lives in such a way as to be spiritually motivated; each day began with a prayer. They did not have a written language; it was within the tribal rituals and symbols that life's mysteries and sacred knowledge were protected and passed down through the generations.

It may have also been their power to search with their minds to intensify an intuitive nature within them that diminished the need for a written language that would have distracted from their unique insight into the world they lived.

Their history reveals a resolute, progressive populace set apart from other Native American Indian Nations and to a great extent sought out as allies by foreign nations. They welcomed the first explorers, traders, and ambassadors of foreign nations that entered their lands, which first brought them prosperity and later adversity. They were highly respected by other Native Indian tribes and usually did not have serious rival adversaries—a superpower, I think.

It seems that as humans progress, nearly every civilization has developed synthetic ways to improve their existence. In most cases, it was at the expense of their personal relationship to an essential universe that supported and guided them—an inner, unique sixth sense they abandoned while escalating dominance over nature and its energies.

For the Wazhazhe, there could be no separation of the secular from the sacred while still preserving balance and Wakonda's blessings.

The setting for the book is on a ranch at the outskirts of the Ouachita Mountain Range north of the Arkansas River. The Ouachita Mountain Range history is nearly all about numerous Native American tribes. The history and legends of the nearby hot springs date back before Europeans arrived on the continent. All trails led to that land of mystery and healing waters. What was it like in its natural grandeur? Little is known except in the stories handed down by the storytellers of the ancestors.

Was the land of the vapors the Garden of Eden or maybe the fountain of youth, or maybe not? It must have been for Native Americans Indians an enormously holy place, the land set aside by the Great Spirit for their spiritual needs. It was a land of mystical beauty, rising steam vapors, herbal plants, mineral mud, and warm therapeutic waters. Today the hills, valleys, cliffs, and springs still whisper of the mystical and restless days gone by.

Part One:

INVITING GLIMPSES INTO THE PAST

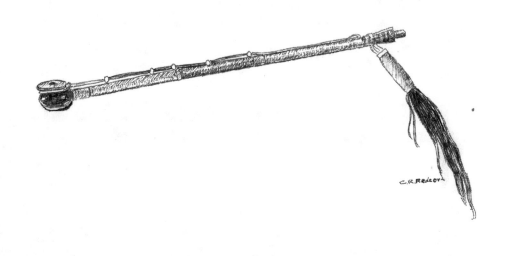

Chapter One:

Children of the middle waters

It was an overcast, rainy day as Sarah and her grandfather, James, drove through the Ouachita Mountains into the valley of their ancestral homestead. The highway wound up and down through the rugged mountains and valleys; Sarah watched to make out the sight of a wild animal, a beautiful plant, or a rushing stream.

At times, it was difficult to see the landscape through the rain and heavy mist that covered the countryside. It did not matter; it only made the trip more exciting and unique, especially since she was with her grandfather.

Sarah was pleased her grandfather had invited her to come with him. She tried to remember when she first visited his studio where he drew sketches and painted pictures of Native American Indian scenes.

She loved to watch the scenes come to life as the lines formed images captivating her thoughts. With each new touch of shading or color, the image became alive with new possibilities for her consideration. Sometimes some of his pictures intrigued her because of how familiar they appeared to her.

Her grandfather's prints of the old west had brought him success and fame as an artist. When Sarah was born his artwork had taken on a more vibrant and realistic appearance. The scenes and images of Native American Indian life just emerged in his mind.

Later he began to realize that with the presence of his granddaughter his work had continually improved, revealing insight beyond his knowledge or experience. His last sketch of an old ranch house could only have been of his family ancestral home.

One night while he was asleep the images, which must have been of his ancestors, began to appear in his mind, giving him the sensation their presence was near and they were forewarning him of something.

The impressions came one after another in a progression he thought would have been of each proceeding generation. He was awakening when the image of his granddaughter, wearing a traditional, ceremonial native Indian dress, appeared.

Now four months later he was returning to his father's birthplace to learn more about his Native Indian heritage and the nature of the images that had mystically appeared to him.

As Sarah watched her grandfather deep in his own thoughts she remembered listening to her father talk about his grandfather Joseph; most of what he said she had not understood, but that did not matter— there was something about her family that made her feel a special way.

Sarah never knew why her grandfather had seldom spoken of or visited the ranch before. It must have been something very secretive and intriguing, maybe even scandalous. She had spent many hours contemplating all the possibilities. Now she had to know more. Unable to restrain her curiosity any longer, she asked her grandfather, "Would you tell me about the ranch and our ancestors?"

Her grandfather smiled and began by telling her, "I do not know much about the ranch or our ancestors either; that is the reason I planned this trip and asked you to come along. Perhaps we can think of this visit in a way that is like being on our own special, secretive adventure to learn more about the ranch and our ancestors together."

"I will tell you what I have learned," he continued. "Most of what I found out about our earlier ancestors, the Wazhazhe Nation, is from what I found in writings of European explorers, books by American Indian authors, and of course American Indian legends. I know now that was not absolutely accurate, and there is much more I would like to know. There was one American Indian author, Francis La Flesche, who I found to be the most reliable; his works came much later.

"The early explorers and traders wrote of their experiences while visiting Wazhazhe villages along the Osage River; only early on our ancestors called themselves Ni-u-kon-ska—the children of the middle water. They did not write much about the Arkansas clans of the Wazhazhe Nation, our ancestors.

"It is remarkable our ancestors did not have a written language at that time; their traditions and history was passed down by their art, songs, and rituals. The songs told of Wakonda, who created the universe and sent the Sky People down to the earth, where they united with the Earth People to become the children of the middle waters."

Sarah had to interrupt. "I have heard about the children of the middle water before; until now I had never thought about the Sky People. Who were they, and where did they come from? It is a myth or just a legend, isn't it?"

James could only respond, "I don't know; at least I am not sure any more. It may have something to do with our ancestors, influential elders called the men of mystery. They thought of the universe as being of two realms or as of two inseparable worlds." Seeing Sarah's interest he continued.

"An invisible world which was the realm of the cause of their being, Wakonda, referred to as something unknown or mysterious. The other realm was that of the visible world we live in, in which all things took a physical form. Everything in the visible world was a reflection of invisible world.

"The men of mystery kept much of their sacred knowledge among themselves and included only a select few to enlighten. I suspect that is why we know very little about them."

Sarah had not heard of this before and had to ask, "The men of mystery who were our ancestors—who were they?" It does not seem possible… the sky people, the men of mystery, and the children of the middle water. Then in their way of thinking it must have been possible to move from one realm to the other like in a myth or a legend?"

James had to laugh. "Well not exactly; I think it was more like in the spiritual or symbolic form it was possible. They believed that the Great Spirit's presence was in all things; it was that spiritual presence that guided and inspired their lives—that is, if they conducted their lives in a righteous manner.

"Somewhere I read about a person who had recently died and their spirit came back in another form like a bird to help their relatives or their clan in some way. There were other spirits recorded as well; the trickster is the most notorious. I know that does not explain the Sky People.

"When I was young only a few families sang the songs, and there were not enough religious leaders to carry out the rituals; only the art work remained. That is why I wanted to become an artist. Maybe all is not lost of our ancestral past way of life if it will live on through you and other descendents."

Sarah asked her grandfather to tell her more about the ancestors.

"Let's see." He sighed. "Our ancestors once followed this very road we are on now, although it was just a trail through the mountains then. Their journey would take them to a place they considered very sacred.

"For some native Indian tribes it was thought to be the Garden of Eden while others thought it to be a special place, a sanctuary given to them by the Great Spirit to provide comfort and cure the sick."

Sarah watched her grandfather's mood change, and then he returned to talking about the ancestors. "Our family, or clan, belonged to a separate branch of the Wazhazhe Nation, the Arkansas, that lived just northeast of where we are now. Every clan had their own leaders, spiritualist, storyteller, and administrative council. Their lives were devoted to learning the purpose and meaning of life and the universe; at least it was until the explorers came from other lands."

When her grandfather had finished, Sarah thought he would have been the storyteller if they lived back then. With some thought she asked, "Grandfather, will you tell me more about my great-grandparents; were they children of the middle water?"

After a moment he said, "Yes, I think so, at least on my side of the family. The children of the middle waters may have been of a way of thinking or that of a unique culture; I don't know. The family, or the clan as your grandmother would say, had a talent for seeing an inner meaning, or symbolic nature, in all things."

Sarah had not ever heard very much about her great-grandparents and with a sigh said, "Tell me more about great-grandfather?"

"There is not a lot I can tell you." He continued. "My father was not one to talk very much. He was a warrior, always away on an assignment or a secret mission somewhere. I only remember he was somehow obligated to be worthy to receive something called the thirteen o-dons; I think that could have been thirteen unique war honors. I did read some of the letters he wrote to your great-grandmother; they were almost like poems.

"I believe many of our ancestors lived just over the mountains to the north along the Buffalo River, near a village that is now a town called Osage. It is not far from the ranch we will visit there before we return home."

Sarah asked, "What of the reservations—why they were not forced to go to the reservations?"

She listened while her grandfather talked. "Unlike other tribes some of your ancestors easily adapted to the changing culture as the settlers from the east expanded into the plains. Not wanting to leave their native land, they welcomed their neighbors and helped them learn the ways of the land.

"They had never fought wars with the federal government, except during the civil war when the clans were divided with some supporting the North while others provided support to the South. Mostly they just made treaties and sent delegations.

"There were others of our family that did go to the new reservation; I do remember hearing about one grandmother. She must have been legendary in her time because my father talked about her as if she was still alive. I expect we will hear more about her at the ranch."

Sarah watched her grandfather as he returned mysteriously into his own thoughts. She had felt a strange sensation come over her as her grandfather talked of the legendary grandmother. Why had she not heard of her before?

This is an extraordinary land, she thought, with the sights and sounds of rain dancing on the rivers and streams while the clouds of mist gave way as if to welcome them into a land of adventure and intrigue. She found herself straining to see around the next bend or down into a valley below.

What of her cousins? Would they be strangers, or even worse, would they be ordinary just like everyone back home? That is what she liked so much about her grandfather: he was not like anyone else. There was a feeling of mystery that surrounded him. Sarah's thoughts returned to the misty rain and images of the fleeting countryside.

A sense of fascination came over Sarah, realizing that the feelings about her grandfather and that of the land they traveled were the same. Was her grandfather coming home, and what of her? She was not of the Bear Clan totally; her mother's family was not even of the Wazhazhe tribe.

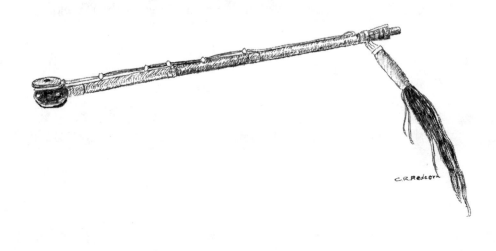

Chapter Two:

Ancestral Ranch and its mysteries

Sarah was stirred from her thoughts as her grandfather turned off the highway onto a narrow gravel lane. We must be on the ranch, she thought, as she searched for any sign of what it would be like. Through the light mist and haze Sarah could scarcely see past the fence that enclosed the roadway.

The road wound through a grove of trees and over a bridge, and then as if by some design a rambling ranch house almost completely surrounded by many building appeared before her. There by one of the buildings Sarah caught a glimpse of someone watching as they drove in.

James, seeing her surprise, said, "This is it, I am sure; this must be the first time you have visited a ranch." Sarah only smiled back; she would tell him later of the feeling that there was someone there who had been waiting for her and that she had realized in some way she might perhaps have been waiting for that one too.

What her grandfather said was true; she had never visited a farm or ranch before—it was all new and exciting. Sarah wanted to remember every detail and was concentrating on not missing anything of her first sight of the ranch when her eyes met those of a most curious looking dog. She could not take her eyes away; in those few seconds nothing else existed, just her and the endless depths within the dog's brown eyes.

A man that was just about her grandfather's age greeted them as they stepped out of the car. After her grandfather introducing himself as a cousin, James, the man welcomed him and said he was his cousin John and had talked to him on the phone. He turned to Sarah, saying, "This is Cousin Hanna. She will show you where to put your things."

Sarah had not noticed her before and wondered where she had come from; Hanna with a quick nod, not looking up, picked up one of Sarah's bags and led the way up stairs into to a small room that looked out onto the mountain range beyond the ranch. Sarah could see the place set aside for her must have been well thought out before. With a knowing look, Hanna merely said, "It is as it should be."

On their way down the stairs Sarah had to ask about the black and white dog she had seen before. Hanna hesitated and then resumed her movement down the stairs, saying nothing. In that brief moment a warm, friendly sensation replaced the curious anxiety that had overwhelmed Sarah. Was she hallucinating or in a dream? She would not ask any more questions—at least not now.

There was much excitement and joy as Sarah met all her cousins except one. Each cousin, from the oldest to the youngest, had to give her their own tour of the ranch and their pets. By the time of the evening meal she was exhausted. Sarah could not help thinking, *it is Hanna—she must be the one that has been waiting for me to come.*

That night some of her cousins had to take her to an old, ghostly and abandoned ranch house hidden some distance away. Hanna only smiled and said, "I must help in the kitchen." Sarah followed her cousins up an overgrown pathway leading past a rundown building that must have been another horse stable and beyond to an old ranch house almost completely falling apart.

Sarah stopped in disbelief; the ranch house was the same as the one in the sketch her grandfather had just finished—except in the sketch it was not falling apart and the moon did not seem so bright and to be hovering overhead to light their way.

Suddenly a glimmer of light danced on the porch of the old house. All her cousins raced away screaming, "The spirit has come back!" Instead of being frightening, there was a warm, inviting presence that invited Sarah to come into the old ranch house.

Sarah made her way up broken steps and across the missing boards of the unstable porch. From inside the house she was sure she could hear the faint voice of someone calling to her.

How silly, she thought. It is only the wind, and it must have been fireflies I saw on the porch. Even so, Sarah thought, could it be the cousins playing tricks on her?

When no one came out, she was sure it was her cousins, but how did they make the fireflies dance that way? It was surely one of the boys. She would not fall for their trick. Her thoughts turned to the one she had only briefly seen when they first arrived.

If there were a mystery about the ranch, it would be that one and the black and white dog with the powerful brown eyes. Somehow the girl, Hanna, was mysterious, too, but not as secret.

Sarah found her grandfather waiting for her near the old horse stables. He explained that her cousins had taken her to the old homestead and had become frightened thinking it was the spirit of an ancestor they believed haunted the old ranch house. She could see he was also taken aback by the resemblance of the buildings to those in his sketches.

As they walked back to join their cousins Sarah held her grandfather's hand, thinking how lucky she was to be with her grandfather and in such an exciting adventure. If only she knew more about her roommate. She had to ask if he could tell her about Hanna.

"If I can," her grandfather answered. "I know her mother caught pneumonia and died when Hanna was four years old. She lived with her grandmother until last year; now she is temporarily living with Cousin John on the ranch. If you want to know more we can talk to him."

"Yes," Sarah said. "Can we talk to him now?"

On their return they found John was waiting for them; he wanted to make sure they didn't need anything before they settled in for the night. It was James who said, "There is; we would like to know more about Hanna."

John replied, "There really is not a lot to tell. Her grandmother was a distant cousin of ours; it was said she lived in this world but was not of this world. For Hanna it must have been very difficult; she had to live in her grandmother's world and conform to the everyday world around her.

"It must be like living in the shadows of both worlds. There is one working on the ranch, a boy named Quinton that seems to understand her."

"There is something else," Sarah said. "There was a black and white dog in the driveway when we arrived. It is the most extraordinary dog I have ever seen. I must know, who does it belong to?"

John began by stating, "You were able to see him. The dog and Quinton, who you probably did not see, are usually together. Where one is the other is close by. Hanna and Quinton are a lot alike in some ways and usually are looking out for each other. No, you probably only surprised Hanna—she may tell you what you want to know after you become better friends."

The next morning Sarah was not able to get Hanna to talk about the old ranch house or anything about the trick played on her; no one mentioned what had happened the night before. That day she spent most of her time with her cousins as they became more acquainted; with all of the things to do, Sarah forgot all about the old ranch house. The animals on the ranch were so much different from those she had come across before. She easily became fond of a horse called Misty.

The horse was born on a misty morning, and everyone just starting calling her Misty. It was alleged the horse was so smart she could unlock gates and get into the best feed and hay. No one rode Misty because she only let Quinton near her. John would only say, "It is her heredity."

This next day Hanna was to show Sarah around the ranch. To their surprise, Misty along with another horse, was saddled and ready to ride. To everyone's horror and then disbelief, except Hanna's, Sarah chose

Misty and easily rode away, thinking, maybe now I will meet Quinton. She did not.

One night just before dawn, Sarah was awakened by a light that filled the room she shared with Hanna. From a window she could see the light had moved along the path to the old ranch house. Deciding not to wake her roommate, she decided to investigate on her own. This time she would catch her mischievous cousins with their tricks.

Sarah traveled up the path, following the light into the old ranch house. She could see the light at the top of a stairway. Sarah managed to climb up a set of rickety old stairs into a room with brightly colored rugs, blankets, and pottery. The light had vanished; instead it was the moon that shined through the window lighting the whole floor.

There were old, faded copies of what looked like more of her grandfather's sketches and artwork hanging on the walls. Draped across a basket stitched tightly together from woven vines and lined with old weathered leather was an old and tattered dress probably worn by someone her age many centuries ago. On top of the dress, she could see a dark blue gemstone just noticeable inside a leather pouch.

That morning at the breakfast table, her grandfather and John were talking about tearing down the old ranch house and horse stables. It was too dangerous to leave the old buildings standing, especially if they were thought to be haunted. John felt more comfortable about tearing down the ancestral home with his cousin James in agreement.

Sarah thought of that morning and the room she had visited. Without thinking, she interrupted the conservation saying, "If there are objects and possessions of such a spirit should we not save them.

"If so, I would willingly help transfer them to a place of safety." It was not that she believed in such things as poltergeist or spirits; the object in the room had in some way influenced her.

"That is a good idea," Cousin John answered. "I believe Hanna would like to help too," he added, knowing that there would no one else to volunteer for the task. The conversation turned to a room in the old horse stables that was said to have been a village leader's house or maybe a council lodge. It would be an ideal place to store the things from the old ranch house.

It would be something like a museum where works of art and other ceremonial artifacts would be displayed. They might even try to create the ceremonies performed for important events and activities like hunting parties and naming ceremonies.

Sarah was up early the next morning helping Hanna with her chores, and later they began the task of searching the old ranch house for anything of value. Sarah slipped the leather pouch into her pocket; she would present it to the family at a more appropriate occasion. By that afternoon they had moved everything they could find from the old ranch house into the big room of the horse stables.

Sarah found a small room, in one corner of the larger room that was probably the council lodge. It was there they placed all the objects removed from the mysterious room she visited the previous morning. When she was organizing the small trunk she discovered four very old paperback books. The pages yellowed, faded, and tattered.

It occurred to her that they might be been someone's journals or maybe a diary and should not be read, at least not yet. It was all so very strange; the light that filled her room and now the journals—if it was a trick being played by her cousins, they were very good, really good.

That evening at the dinner table, it was agreed upon that the old stables would be removed and to restore the single room in the middle to a council lodge. There was much discussion about how to refurbish the room until one cousin spoke. "I have read about the houses of our ancestors." He began by showing them some drawings he had made from the books he had read.

All along the exterior of the single room large saplings were driven into the ground then bent over and tied at the top. Along the walls and roof smaller saplings were interwoven between the larger saplings, and the framework was covered with sheets of bark or woven mats. There were openings in the roof for the smoke from the fires to escape.

"By now the saplings must have rotted off in the ground," he said. "We should restore inside the room to its original appearance but reinforce the framework with timbers that would change its outward appearance only slightly."

As her older cousin talked, Sarah remembered what her grandfather had said about the family living in the shadows of a spiritual one. There was an element of mystery about the family but to believe in a spiritual one like in a shaman; that was a little hard to accept as true even with the old, abandoned ranch house, the sketches, and the mysterious light.

What about the girl, Hanna? Sarah looked around the room; Hanna had left without anyone noticing. With a long and very loud yawn she rose from her chair and excused herself; she had to know more about Hanna and of Hanna's grandmother.

Hanna was in her room waiting for Sarah. "Is there something you would like to know from me?" Hanna asked.

"Yes", Sarah replied, "but first I must know what cousin John meant when he said your grandmother lived in this world but was not of this world."

"I cannot tell you what he meant; only think of the first day you came to the ranch—you were not of the ranch. Still today you are not of the ranch, but you live on the ranch. It was the way of my grandmother and those of many generations before."

Sarah thought for a moment and responded, "You are saying even though I am staying on the ranch I do not think of myself as being part of this ranch. Okay, fair enough. Are you sure you are only twelve? Tell me more about your grandmother: did she talk about the ancestors, the sky people, and of an invisible world?"

Hanna started to speak, hesitated, and then said, "Please, you must excuse me, I have not talked this much before. It is not that I do not want to tell you. It is difficult to place in words; you are asking about things that cannot be explained, only experienced."

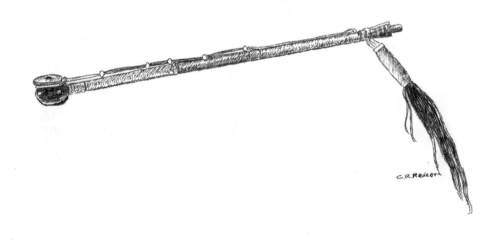

Chapter Three:

The Journals:
"A mystifying influence"

By the next morning Sarah could not resist looking at the journals. She had to know who wrote them and how old they were. She discovered the journals were written in a hand she could not make out and marked with symbols she did not understand. Sarah dusted off an old rocking chair that she thought should have fallen apart long ago and sat down. Carefully she examined the journals. The first one was definitely a diary, she thought, similar in style to her own diaries.

She was ready to give up then she remembered what her grandfather's cousin John had said about Hanna: "She had to live in her grandmother's world and conform to the everyday world around her."

If that was so then Hanna would probably know what the symbols and writing was all about; but then what if the journals were made up just to play a trick on her and Hanna? Someone could easily copy the symbols and writing from some book. Either way she wanted to know.

At first Hanna was reluctant to help with the journals but then as if given permission began to explain what the symbols and letters were about. After some time Hanna determined that on the front cover of the first journal was written "The Mysterious Gift."

She reasoned the next two journals were more like the memoirs of four companions as they journeyed into different adventures. As they studied the journals, Sarah knew she must let her grandfather know what she had discovered.

All the rest of the day Sarah's grandfather was occupied with his cousin and others of the clan as they planned for the renovation of the council lodge. Word of their intentions had reached other relatives who could come on weekends to lend a hand. The only question remaining was the old ranch house: should it be renovated or torn down? It was a subject no one wanted to talk about, and the matter was set aside.

Later that day Sarah had made her mind up that the journals belonged to all the family and that she wanted to reveal their discovery during dinner. Once again she found that Hanna became silent but did not disagree. Sarah expected the family to be excited and full of curiosity; instead a silence fell over everyone. Sarah wondered what she had done wrong. John was the first to speak.

"It is not you, Sarah," he said. "It was my mother's wish that everything in her room was not to be disturbed. Some of our family believe it is my mother's spirit that has haunted the old ranch house, keeping her room just as she left it. Once I went into her room to silence the talk; a feeling that I should not be there came over me, and I left."

He continued, "It seems that everything has changed now that you have come to the ranch. It is as it should be that you have found the journals; it is obvious she meant for you and Hanna to have the journal and her special things. They are yours to do with what you like. I believe it will be all right to tear down the old ranch house now."

Sarah was still a bit puzzled; okay just for obvious reasons how the spirit, if that is what it was, knew she was coming to the ranch. The words of her grandfather once again occupied her thoughts: "They believed that the Great Spirit's presence was in all things; it was that spiritual presence that guided and inspired their lives. That is if they conducted their lives in a righteous manner."

It still did not make any sense unless there were two inseparable, parallel worlds—two different realms. There could be other spirits as well like the one that haunting the old ranch house. No, that was impossible.

Although who was it that called to her from inside the old ranch house? She now knew her cousins would not have been inside, especially at night. How could she explain the fireflies? They were real enough. And Cousin John saying everything had changed now—changed from what?

Sarah was determined to unravel the mystery surrounding her grandfather, the family, and the ranch. She needed to know more about the family, especially her great-grandfather. The journal, if it was real, possible could tell her about him and about the family living in the shadows of a spiritual one.

The next day Sarah was left alone with the journals; Hanna had suddenly disappeared, and her other cousins reluctant to join her where their great-grandmother was concerned. It did not matter; it was an adventure she would share with Misty.

On this morning ride she discovered a beautiful place on the river where a rock formation spanned nearly all the way across the river.

There she found a comfortable place overlooking the water as it fell from the rock formation; with some reservations and a great deal of eagerness she took

out the journal from the saddle bag and began to examine it. As she began to grasp the veiled meaning of the symbols, each phrase became more easily understood; soon she was making sense of the journal with very little difficulty.

"Oh," Sarah murmured, "yes, it is a medley of English and French … nothing like I studied in school though."

She stopped reading; as she let her mind grasp what she had discovered, a feeling came over her that there was a mysterious influence about the journal, one that was in some way guiding her. It seemed to her that the words sprang from the journal with an essence of their own. The mysterious influence she experienced only increased her need to discover more.

Sarah heard Misty give out a welcoming whinny; the black and white dog she had seen at the driveway the day she arrived was coming up to her. Her first thought was, *if you see the dog then the one called Quinton is around somewhere.* She was certain now that he must have been the one she caught a glimpse of that first day, although she could not see him now.

It dawned on Sarah that she had been riding his horse, now his dog was lying in front of her, and she had not even met him. It was all a little confusing and highly incredible to her. If Quinton was around, maybe the dog would lead her to him; to her surprise the dog rose up gave an acknowledging bark and ran a short distance away.

Sarah was not sure if it was her or the horse, Misty, that the dog was expecting to follow. She quickly mounted Misty and said, "Okay, what are you thinking now?" This time Misty gave out a gentle whinny and softly repositioned Sarah left boot a little farther away from a tender spot. *Okay*, Sarah thought, *why don't both of you take me to see the elusive one, Quinton.* With that the dog began a slow trot with Misty close behind.

For a while they followed the river into a valley that wound through the mountain range. Sarah could see the faint appearance of smoke drifting up from within a canyon further ahead. She gave Misty a gentle pat on the side of her neck when they turned into the gap leading into the canyon. Sarah thought, *I must be entering a different era, a place time must have passed by.*

Misty quickened her pace and caught up to the dog that had stopped before an open fireplace set alone on a raised area of rock. "So I should get down you are thinking," Sarah whispered to Misty, not quite believing what she had just said. Once more to Sarah's bewilderment Misty moved to a spot where she could easily dismount onto the rock formation near the fireplace.

A little while later Sarah could hear the chatter of what sounded like very unhappy animals of some kind; then she heard "Do not be alarmed—it is only two bothersome raccoons fighting over some sunflower seeds I spilled." Sarah turned to see someone replacing Misty's bridle with a halter, saying, "Do not worry. The horse will come back; they like to go down by the stream, and the bridle makes it difficult for her to drink or eat grass and things."

Sarah could barely reply. "You must be Quinton? Thank you for sending your dog to me and letting me ride your horse." Quinton was not at all like she expected. Even though he was dressed like a ranch hand, he was not—she was sure of that.

"I am not the one you should be thanking," Quinton replied, "although I did saddle Misty the day you first went riding… it was a premonition, I guess. The dog, Tip, pretty much does what he wants, and so does Misty. If you feed her and brush her once a day she will take you where you want to go."

"Where are we?" Sarah asked. "I have never been in a place like this before." It was obvious that Quinton was not there looking for stray cows. There was something else; she could not figure out what.

"Not many have," Quinton said in almost a sigh. "I am a little surprised you found your way here. Now that you have I must ask you not to tell anyone about it. It is why I am working on the ranch and why I could not meet you before."

"You have not explained what you are doing here," Sarah said. "I will not tell anyone except for my grandfather, but only if it is necessary, and maybe Hanna, if you tell me what you are doing here."

Quinton started to leave and changed his mind, saying, "If that is a promise then, I am looking for the little people. I am an anthropologist; my studies of the little people have brought me to the ranch and to this valley. There, I have told you. Now will you keep your promise and not tell anyone?"

"Of course," Sarah said with a smile, thinking, *what little people? What is he talking about? He seemed so intelligent and normal before. I guess being an anthropologist you have to explore all possibilities.* She had to ask, "Why do you think there are little people in this valley?"

"I do not know for certain," Quinton said. "This is where my research has led me, and the signs are here. If the stories and legions about the little people are true, you should not be riding alone in these mountains. You had better go back now. Hanna, she is waiting for you I think." Sarah turned to see Misty standing once again where she could easily climb on.

"You do not need the bridle," Quinton said, inviting her to ride with only the halter. "Remember your promise, especially about this fire."

CHAPTER FOUR:

THE MYSTERIOUS GIFT

Quinton was right. Sarah did not need the bridle on the ride back to the ranch house; Misty seemed to know her every need before she did. It all seemed so unreal to Sarah; first Hanna, then the mysterious events at the old ranch house, next there was Quinton, and what about his horse and dog? No! Quinton was right—it was not like they belonged to him or anyone else.

Sarah began to remember what her grandfather had said in the car on their way to the ranch; it was that perhaps they could think of their visit in a way that was like being on their own special, secretive adventure to learn more about the ranch and their ancestors together. For a moment she questioned why her grandfather had said that, then dismissed it as just a coincidence.

What was most disturbing was that in some way everything seemed to involve her, and that was the most intriguing mystery of all. For a moment her thoughts turned to Hanna. What of Hanna? In some way she was part of the mysterious influence that surrounded the family; in some way Hanna was like a mirror of herself reflecting her most hidden thoughts.

"Okay, Misty," she whispered, "Let's just see; take me back to the ranch house." Sarah removed the journal from the saddle bag, turned back to the front page, and spoke the words, "The Mysterious Gift." Listen up, Misty," she whispered and began to read out loud; there was no one close to hear her.

It is the Year 1915. There is a quiet serenity about the land like that just before a storm—the undercurrents of time gone by and that which is to come.

It is the occasion of their fourteenth year; winter's chilly grip has finally giving way to warm, southwest winds that flow all through the ridges and valleys of the Ouachita Mountain Range. The winter has been long and bitter this year. No one had anticipated the coming of spring more than Joseph.

For Joseph life has always been simple: he occupies his days roaming his family's cattle ranch nestled between the Arkansas River and the edges of the dense Ouachita Mountain woodland forest.

Someday he would take his place with his father and older brothers in working the family ranch, but until then he only wanted to relive the life of native Indian warriors and to be part of nature as his ancestors were long ago.

His father had forbidden him to journey into the rugged Ouachita Mountains alone until his fourteenth birthday. That day is almost here.

Moonlight still shimmered into his room as Joseph quietly dressed and slipped out of his family's ranch house. Sometime in the night, he was aroused from sleep by the shrieks of a wild animal. He had drifted back asleep only to experience the sound re-emerging in his consciousness.

The shrieks had to come from a large cat, maybe a bobcat, he thought. He was still trying to understand why a bobcat came this close to the ranch house when he decided to investigate.

Joseph knew if he wanted to track the bobcat back to its lair, he would have to be out before dawn. The light of the moon was bright that night, and he should be able to see the bobcat's trail. He begins searching the rolling hills above the house then circled around to the Little Piney River, which flowed out of the mountains and through the ranch.

A feeling of triumph overcame him as he found a set of paw marks. All the great warriors from before must be looking down on him with pride, he thought.

Soon after Joseph began to follow the bobcat's trail, another set of paw marks appeared. They were the same size and shape, but something was not right. Further up the river he discovered a set of prints that were much larger than the first two.

The tracks were definitely not from a bobcat. Like a flash of light, he realized he was following a cougar with her two cubs. The mother cougar must have been watching him as her two cubs traveled back to their lair. Joseph shuddered as a cold chill passed through him, but he could not give up.

Further up the trail Joseph determined the cougar was stopping only long enough for her cubs to travel ahead. He knew he was out of any danger because protecting her cubs was her only concern. What never entered his mind was that the mother cougar might have considered him a cub too.

With each step, he was venturing into part of the mountain range in which he had never been before. He was both surprised and excited as the cougar traveled through a pass into a canyon within the mountains.

The canyon opened up into a valley concealed by high cliffs and tall tree formations.

A lush meadow spread out beyond the sides of a gentle stream overflowing with wildlife undisturbed by his presence. Sunlight was just beginning to filter over the mountain, as Joseph stood at the valley entrance too overwhelmed to continue.

He could see the big cat with her two cubs drinking from a spring near the edge of a cliff. In his mind, he mapped out the spring water as it traveled down an embankment into a small brook. This was the best place to hunt or set traps along the stream.

His thoughts turned to the big cat. Why had she allowed him to follow her to the valley? He had read of such places in the books of his native Indian ancestors. In such a site as this one, they wrote of Wakonda, a great spirit or a great mystery, who created the universe. The spiritual presence of Wakonda protected all forms of life from harm.

That would account for the way the cougar and all the other animals in the valley behaved. Joseph shrugged off the stories about a Great Spirit and decided he would keep the valley in mind next winter when he went hunting.

As he stood looking into the valley, its peacefulness overcame him, and he became occupied with the rhythms of the scene and the alluring melodies he was hearing; in his mind he begin to transform the sounds into a chant.

Who has brought me to this valley,
a cry in the night?
The cougar led the way
to bring me to this native land.
She drinks from the stream without fear;
why does she not realize the hunter that I am?

Who has brought me to this valley,

nature's mysteries?

The cougar led the way

to awaken me to this native land.

She is not what she seems;

an apparition or prophecy she must be.

Who has brought me to this valley,

spirits in night?

The cougar led the way

to consider this native land.

Why have I been chosen?

A believer in spirits I am not.

Joseph stepped back, shaking his head. He must not let himself venture into the world his sister entertains. Just then, he remembered his father had told him he wanted him to be home before the midday meal. It probably had something to do with his birthday.

By the time he came into the kitchen, all his family had finished eating and were going about their daily routines. His mother was accustomed to him coming in late and had left a plate of food for him.

As he ate, he could hear the delicate movement of his twin sister, as she entered the room. Ida Belle sat down across the table from him, waiting for him to finish eating. Joseph glanced across the table, questioning his sister's intentions. She reminded him of the cougar that watched him from the spring.

From the day they were born, she could feel his every emotion. Joseph knowing it would be useless to avoid telling her everything related his encounter with the cougar, even though it was his inclination not to.

As Joseph talked, Ida Belle closed her eyes, allowing his voice to convey images into her thoughts. She could picture the mountain spring as it flowed into the stream with hundreds of plants, some herbs, growing along the banks.

Around the stream, she could visualize the animals as they watched the reflection of the moonlight dancing on the surface of the lake. Ida Belle could see the sun rising above the mountains. As the first beams of light from the sun reached the moon's mirror image, the animals began to disappear.

Ida Belle sat back in her chair; the chant of her brother kept reverberating in her mind, but she would think of it no more. Her father's relatives were to come and stay with them for the summer; she would ask her great-grandmother to explain the visions.

As she watched Joseph finish his meal, she thought how different they were. Her brother seldom talked and preferred to be alone while she found life and its mysteries both intriguing and inspirational.

She wonders, Who is this twin brother of mine, the one who strives to be a hunter or warrior worthy of his ancestors? He is like the cougar he tracks—calm and collected on the outside while fierce and spirited inside. In the English books he reads, is he the inventor or explorer. He will not be the rancher or farmer as is his father. It is in his chant I believe; he cannot escape the spirit of his ancestors.

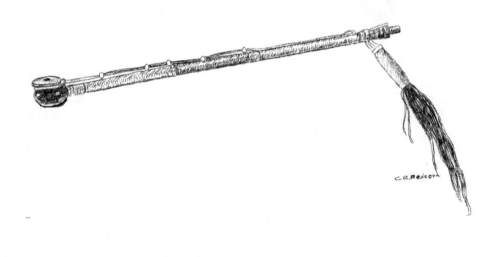

Part Two:

A CURIOUS PRESENCE

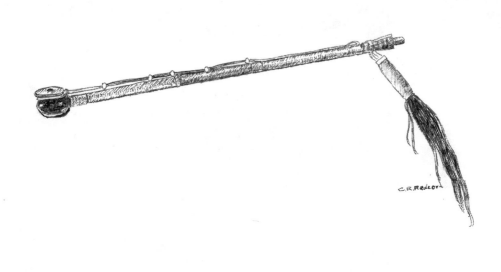

Chapter Five:

A natural order

Sarah stopped reading when Misty slowed to cross a small stream. Her mind returned to the first two paragraphs; she was convinced more than ever that the journal was part of a trick. Why would whoever wrote the journal write it in a way that spoke to her, if they were writing it for themselves?Misty had crossed the stream, so she began to read again.

It was late in the afternoon as Joseph watched anxiously for his father to come back to the ranch. At last, he could see his father's team of horses turning onto the narrow, winding road leading up to the house. He did not want his father to see how impatient he was. Just then, it came to him: it was a good time for him to sweep the front porch for his mother.

When he was finished, his father was coming up the walk followed by an oddly colored dog. It was not the kind of dog

Joseph expected. It was not a dog for hunting; maybe it was a herding dog. He did not understand, because on the ranch they only used horses to work the cattle.

This dog was not large enough to survive in the forest. It would have been better if it were a dog for hunting raccoons or better yet one to hunt mountain lions and bears. As his mind raced to find the answer for the strange dog's presence, he sat back on the porch swing. Feeling his son's discomfort, his father sat down beside him.

Filled with curiosity the dog, a cattle dog, lay down in front of the swing with his big brown eyes fixed on the boy. He had always known humans looked at the universe different than canines, and they had unique skills, which made them special in some way. As a pup, he found it almost impossible to communicate with humans unless it was about them.

There was something about this boy; he would be different. As their eyes met, something deep within their sub-consciousness emerged, and the awareness of a time long ago awakened between them. The familiarity of past generations momentarily returned; an elusive awareness would remain.

Before long the man said, "Our family has lived on this land for many generations. You know it has always been our livelihood to raise cattle and horses. Joseph, there is a great war going on in another land. It looks like the government will get us into the war. Soon your older brothers may have to join the army. You may have to take on some of their work now and become more responsible."

Joseph's first thought was of warriors protecting their village from invading nomadic tribes or a war party protecting their ancestral hunting grounds. The notion of his older brothers fighting in a war disturbed Joseph. What did they know about being warriors? They were very good at ranching and knew a lot about raising crops. Had they not given up the ways of their Indian ancestors?

What had his father just said now? In the morning, there will be a herd of goats coming to the ranch. It was to be his responsibility to manage the goats. Jack, the border collie, will help him handle the goats.

Joseph felt his life was over. He could not imagine his life without being out in the wild outdoors with the birds and animals, free to do what he wanted when he wanted. The idea of taking care of goats made everything worse.

How much help would this dog be taking care of goats? He would rather have a horse to help him. He tried to concentrate on what his father was saying. The goat herd would provide meat and clear the valleys of brush to make more grazing land for the cattle.

Joseph mind visualized the goats going everywhere; how could he manage to keep them from running off? Joseph In his dilemma had not noticed the horse tied behind his father's wagon.

"Joseph!" His father raised his voice, well aware his son was immersed in his own thoughts. "See if you can do anything with the new horse I came by today. I don't suspect that horse will ever learn to work with cattle. It must be her color.

"She looks more like an Indian pony than a roper. Everyone has given up on her. The whole county is talking about her. They called her Sadie, I think. Maybe you can find some use for her. You will find her tied behind the wagon."

Joseph had heard about Sadie from his friends at school. He could not believe his good fortune. It did not matter if Sadie was not good at working cattle. Her color is perfect. Most of her body is tan and white. Her face and feet are white except for one eye that was tan. What Joseph liked best of all is the tan spots on her white hips and chest.

Joseph's attention turned from the pony to the goat herd. He had gone from very few responsibilities to having a horse and a dog and taking care of a goat herd. Just then, he thought of the dog that was to help him.

He would never question his father, but how could one dog protect the goat herd from the wild animals especially a cougar or even a bear? What was he called… Jack? His father had said the cattle dog was his responsibility.

Jack was aware that the boy had begun to look at him in a different way. He watched as the boy removed supplies from the wagon. At first, Jack did not understand when the boy said "heel," but he decided he would follow him. He would remember the boy's body movements and the sound "heel."

The boy led him to a large building where there was a familiar smell of horses, feed, and hay. Jack examined every detail of the structure as he followed the boy down a long alleyway that enclosed a large inner room from the outer horse stalls. There was something about the inner room that puzzled Jack; nothing hostile or harmful—it was more like the suggestion of a familiar memory.

Before long, they came to two stalls that joined a large door leading out into a small pasture behind the stables. At the side of one of the stalls there was an empty space; Jack concluded the boy had selected this area for him to stay. Jack watched the boy as he returned to the ranch house. Somehow, he felt both a responsibility and devotion to the boy and his ranch.

Later on, the cattle dog watched the boy lead the horse into a stall across from him. The horse was not like any he had been around before; this horse had noticed him at once without showing any signs of concern. Jack had become use to other ranch animals always having misgivings about him.

Somewhere, lost in time, it had become the responsibility of all dogs to provide a sense of balance between humans and the animal world. He did not mind, because in the physical world it was his job to help the ranchers manage the other animals. It just made his job easier if the other animals understood there would be no nonsense while he was around.

Jack was right: Sadie was different. She had never been satisfied doing the things expected of a ranch horse. How could they expect her to stop thinking for herself just because a rider was on her back? She would be perfectly content working with the ranchers if they allowed her to think about some things for herself.

When the boy brought her from the wagon, she felt no uneasiness or nervousness in the boy; maybe this ranch would be okay. She was very content as the boy fed and brushed her, not being used to such care, and gave out a low whinny every time the boy found the exact spot to brush.

Still, there was the dog, unlike any she had ever seen before today, probably a cattle dog, Why was he in the stables with her? Sadie did not object to the dog. She liked having a companion and a dog might be of some use.

Joseph had placed Sadie in a stall next to the large room still standing just as it was built centuries before. Today the room had become the tack room housing everything needed to take care of horses.

The tack room had always been a special place for Joseph. For generations this room was the center of all activities. In one corner was a smaller room, hidden away and forbidden by folklore to enter. The small room had often startled Joseph because he could sometimes feel a curious presence there.

Still the tack room was where he would go when he wanted to be alone or was working out a difficult problem. He could get absorbed in the smell of leather and become enticed by pictures that invited him to visit the past. His favorite photograph was of his great-grandmother dressed in her native Wazhazhe Indian clothes.

Joseph favored time of the day had always been during the evening meal—that is, if he did not have to speak. The whole family would talk about what had happened that day. Sometimes the conservation would include their relatives and upcoming events.

He was certain there would be talk of the goat herd and, without saying it directly, what his new responsibilities would be. Reluctantly he went back to the house.

Jack had just settled in for the night when he heard the soft steps of a young girl coming into the horse stables. He had noticed her and an older woman in the house while he was on the porch. Unexpectedly, Jack found himself surrounded by a mystical energy as the girl leaned down to smooth the hair over his eyes and around his ears.

Chapter Six:

The trickster: "an invisible world"

As the night turned into morning Jack began to explore his new home. After inspecting all the buildings and the surrounding area, he picked a spot suitably concealed that would have a good view of the house, stables, and surrounding landscape.

It was a strange land with mountains, trees, and rivers everywhere. It was impossible for him to tell where the valley ended as it turned in so many directions. He had come from the land of the big sky and the rolling grasslands of the prairie.

On the prairie, the sounds and smells carried a long distance, and he was always able to tell from what and where they came. In the land of the tall trees, he would have to be on guard at all times.

Jack turned his attention to the ranch house. He could smell the aroma of what the humans called bacon and fresh bread. Once a man had given him bacon; it sure was good. He would never forget that sound, "bacon."

He watched as the boy and girl came out of the house. To his surprise the girl came up to his hideaway with bacon and bread covered with something that tasted very good. He would have liked to stay a while with her but knew he should follow the boy.

Sadie became excited when she heard the boy coming. It is the first time she experienced the friendship of any human. Even with the other horses, she often felt alone and abandoned. As the boy came into the stable, she gave out a low, whinnying sound.

Jack could only watch with curiosity as the boy and the horse formed an attachment with each other. It might be all right for a boy and a horse but not for a hardworking cattle dog like himself; that was indisputable.

He was feeling a little left out when the boy called, "Jack!" He heard the sound heel; *it was time for him to go to work.* Very good, *Jack thought, hopeful there would not be any foolishness like* sit *or worst of all* roll over. *If they were going to handle cattle, the boy would have to know what he was doing.*

Joseph guided Jack down a pathway that led him through trees, past a water basin, and into an open meadow. Jack almost wished he could explore on his own when the boy began giving him familiar commands. First, he was to go forward, then go left, no, go right. He did not see any cattle… what was the boy doing?

The next command sent him right into a hideous possum. Jack, completely at a loss, thought the boy was sending him to herd a little hairy creature. The possum fell over on its back with all four feet straight up in the air. It was all puffed up with its tongue hanging out the side of its mouth. Jack could hardly endure the smell. It was the smell of ill will.

He had heard of a mischievous spirit, the trickster; that sometimes takes on the appearance of an animal or another form to play tricks on humans. Jack stepped back, knowing that if it was the trickster it had the ability to defy both time and space and escape into the invisible world.

Jack knew humans had long ago lost their understanding of the supernatural world where the trickster dwells in. There was no doubt this was the trickster. He could only stand there trying to understand what would cause the magical one to appear here and now.

Joseph ran as fast as he could to find out what was happening. Once there his heart almost stopped beating. The border collie was supposed to be a herding dog, not to hunt and kill possums. What would he tell his father? His father had trusted him to watch over the dog. He just knew he would be working with goats the rest of his life.

Joseph's attention turned to the possum. He thought it was dead but realized its face was wrinkled up as if it was grinning. There were not any

wounds or marks anywhere. Jack watched as the boy leaned over the possum to get a better look.

When he could not take it any longer, Jack let out a sharp warning, forcing the boy away from the possum. Both Joseph and Jack stood motionless, caught up in a dilemma neither one could control. In an instant, the trickster disappeared before them into the invisible world from which it had come.

In the same instant, Joseph caught a glimpse into the supernatural world of apparitions. He tried to make sense out of the affair by repeating the events over in his mind. There was something strange and mystical about the way the possum behaved. Could it have moved that fast? Why did he not see it leave? It was as if someone had played a trick on him. He could not believe it was the possum.

Still trying to make sense out of what just happened, he began walking on to the corral with Jack by his side. They soon came in sight of the livestock corrals. There were buildings full of hay, wooden grain bins, and a gentle flowing stream. Jack knew this would be his home forever.

That was until a herd of goats could be heard coming up the lane. Joseph looked down questioningly at the cow dog stretched out on the ground with both his paws over his eyes. It was obvious to Jack that it was going to be his job to help the boy with goats.

Jack opened his eyes to see a large, white dog begin to lead the goats away from him. He had heard of the large, white dogs call Great Pyrenees. They were working dogs that protected sheep and goats from wolves, bears, and other wild animals. This one was beautiful and about his age. Jack at once appreciated the way she moved and was protecting the goats.

He decided to move closer to get a better look. As he did, a bark that sounded like thunder stopped him instantly. It was another Great Pyrenees rising up out of the middle of the goat herd. Jack stepped back startled, as the second Pyrenees towered over the goat herd. He understood at once that would be the only warning the big dog would give him.

Just then, he heard Joseph give him commands that must have been to herd the goats into a corral. For one second Jack considered the big white dog. He was used to taking care of large bulls; he was not afraid. To Jack's surprise, the Great Pyrenees followed the goats into the corral.

Joseph had been watching to see how the dogs would get along. There should not be a problem with the female dog or Jack, but what about the big male dog? His thoughts then turned to the two drovers that herded the goats from the New Mexico territory. They had agreed to stay through the night while the goats became used to the ranch.

The drovers helped him bring feed and water into the corral. When the goats had all been taken care of, they began to give Joseph advice on how to take care of the goat herd. The goats would not be a problem as long as they were with the Pyrenees dogs and they were free to come back to their corral. He only needed to drive them to graze in the morning and make sure they returned before dusk. He was in no way to touch or feed the Pyrenees dogs.

Joseph thought of how he must interact with the border collie as he returned to the horse barn. Before today, he thought cattle dogs were limited to herding livestock. Now, he was not so sure. There was a lot more to this border collie than he had expected. The border collie had warned him about the possum. Besides, this is the first dog that ever looked straight into his eyes. He did not forget his father relied on him not to spoil the cattle dog.

When Joseph reached the stables, he could hear his mother and younger sister moving furniture around in the ranch house. He had almost forgotten his great-grandmother was coming to visit them in two days. The room next to his was to become his great-grandmother's room. He did not know much about her.

Joseph thought of the picture of his grandmother when she was young in her native Wazhazhe Indian dress. It surprised him how much the picture looked like him, except for the dress and being a girl. She must look a lot different now. From an upstairs window his mother called to him, "Joseph, bring Grandmother's wooden basket from the forbidden room."

Joseph found the basket easily. He had come across the basket last winter while searching the storeroom for something to do. Unable to control his curiosity, he had looked into the forbidden room. There on a dusty shelf he could see a medicine pipe and many objects that he could not tell what they were.

Just within reach, a basket stitched tightly together from woven vines and lined with buffalo or elk hides appeared out of place and needed to

47

be rearranged. Through the small splits in the woven vines, he could see unfamiliar symbols and writing.

Joseph, as if in a spell, had reached out to straighten the basket. For an instant, he could not let go as a time long ago flashed through his mind. He had asked his mother about the basket. She said she did not know except a legend said the basket could only be handed down to one who is gifted. The basket was there when she came to the ranch. He should not have touched it without permission.

"Joseph!" His sister called as she entered the tack room. "You had better hurry. Mother is waiting for the basket. Mother said we should call Great-grandmother by her childhood name Warmwind. Do you know she is over one hundred years old? I heard Mother say she had asked to leave the reservation especially to see us.

"I wonder why. "

Joseph just shook his head and carried the basket out of the tack room.

On the way to the house, Joseph smiled as he remembered all the rumors he had heard about his great-grandmother. They could not have been true. His sister's question was interesting. Why did she want to come see the two of them? It probably was not important. Anyway, there were things to think about that were more important.

Ida Belle took the basket from her brother and brought it into the room being prepared for Warmwind. She was pleased with the brightly colored rugs, blankets, and pictures that decorated the room. In some mysterious way, she felt the presence of her great-grandmother already in the room.

Joseph tried not to think about his great-grandmother and gifted ones as he hurried back to the tack room. He took time to give Sadie an apple before going into the tack room. This time he left the door open for Jack to come in with him. The dog was good company and was more like a friend than a ranch animal.

Jack watched inquisitively as Joseph assembled a blanket saddle and a rope bridle. When finished the bridle consisted of a single rope with a loop that would fit comfortable in Sadie's mouth. The saddle was even more curious—it was a heavy blanket with clasps on one side and straps on the other.

When Jack looked around the room, he noticed a picture of a human on his horse looking out over a wooded valley from a hilltop. There was something very similar to the saddle and bridle the boy had made. This was very confusing; how could the boy capture it all and place it in the glass?

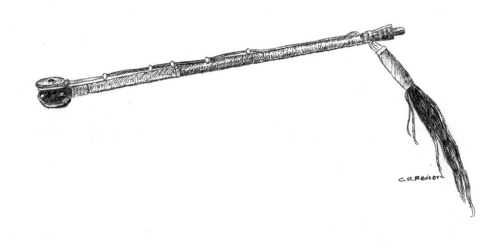

Chapter Seven:

A new order in the land

The next morning Jack was up before dawn. A powerful feeling that someone was watching him had come over him in the night. He searched the stables, around the house, and down by the stream but did not find anything.

Satisfied, he returned to the same place he had selected the day before. He sniffed the aroma coming from the house; it smelled just like something a man had given him that he called a sourdough pancake.

As the girl came out of the house, pancake in hand, it took all his will power to control his excitement. Unable to control the sensation, he ran out to meet her. Soon she was scratching him and soothing him with her songs. Just as Jack became completely under her spell, the boy came out of the house.

Joseph was carrying food and other provisions for the drovers as he left the house. He only looked once toward the border collie completely under the influence of his twin sister. The border collie quickly finished his pancake and followed the boy into the horse stables. They stopped only long enough to move Sadie into a larger corral before going on to the goat corral.

The border collie had noticed the boy's disapproving behavior, and he was determined to regain his self-respect. Was it not his job to take care of the boy? Today he would stay well ahead of the boy as they traveled down the lane to the livestock corrals. At first, the boy tried to move ahead, but it was no use. Jack was quite satisfied with himself; the boy obviously had underestimated his abilities.

Joseph and Jack arrived at the goat corral just as the drovers had finished loading their packhorses. After eating they were ready to return home but agreed to watch over the boy and his collie as they moved the goats out to forage.

They were surprised how efficiently with the boy's command the border collie moved the goats out of the corral and into the open valley. The Great Pyrenees began to scout ahead of the herd, making sure it was safe, while the border collie moved the goat at the boy's commands.

Only the Great Pyrenees was aware of the struggle that was beginning to emerge between the boy and the cow dog. When the goat herd reached the grazing area, Joseph signaled for Jack to return.

On their return to the stables, there was still the sense of competition between them, even though the bond of friendship and competition would make them perpetual companions. Still, there was the horse Sadie; they must include her even though they did not know why.

Upon entering the stables, Jack once again had the sensation of an intruder watching them. This time he knew he was not mistaken as he searched the stables. He searched the hayloft, the horse stalls, and the corrals outside the stables without finding the source of his impressions. Jack returned as the boy was coming out of the tack room with the bridle and saddle adapted just for the horse.

Jack pondered the situation as the boy showed the horse his custom-made riding gear. It was clear the boy and horse were anxiously trying to do their best. He noticed how easily the horse allowed the boy to place the blanket on her back and gently buckle the attached straps. He was sure there would be a problem when the boy placed the rope around her lower jaw; then the horse turned her head and gave a low whinny as if to give the boy encouragement.

Sadie did want to give the boy encouragement; her response was more of a question. Without stirrups, how was the boy going to get on her back? Sadie waited patiently as the boy became aware of the challenge and led her to a low rock wall. The moment the boy was on her back Sadie could feel his youthful touch.

As he leaned forward, she instinctively moved ahead. Sadie felt the boy become confident as she responded to his movements. At first, her moves were slow but sure. Then she began to respond more rapidly, making sure the boy was in control. Before long, they were racing through the valley and through the streams.

At first, Jack tried to keep up with the boy on his horse. When that did not work, he tried to predict what the boy and his horse would do next. Unable to carry on, he gave up and began to move from one hilltop to the next, keeping them in sight. He could not let this happen. The boy had found a way to overcome his speed and strength. In a moment of intense rivalry, Jack leaped onto Sadie's back

Suddenly the three companions experienced a new freedom of venture and unbound possibilities. Each with their own individual personalities and traits, they had come together to defy boundaries and their own limitations.

Joseph urged Sadie to follow the flight of a golden eagle flying ahead of them. The eagle had just swooped down and snatched a huge snake from the ground in front of them. The eagle with some difficulty flew toward a rock formation that stretched into the mountains and above the tree line, the snake being its only worry.

Sadie followed the eagle until it dropped the snake onto the rock formation over again many times. Then the eagle flew into a nest high into the trees along the mountain ledges. Joseph climbed to a place overlooking the eagle's nest with Jack right behind.

Together they watched the eagle feeding its young, with Sadie watching from the ground below. Sadie had waited patiently for Joseph and Jack to come down from ledge above. Finally she gave out a very loud and long whinny that alerted the eagle of their presence. Both Joseph and Jack raced down the rocks just ahead of the eagle.

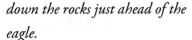

Joseph reached a narrow opening in the rock formation, where Sadie was waiting, only moments before the eagle reached him. Sadie waited only long enough for Joseph to climb on; then she sprinted into the trees moments before the eagle dove down again, screeching her disapproval.

When all was clear the three soul mates found their way to the hidden valley Joseph had found two days before. While Jack and Sadie drank from the pool below the spring, Joseph found a patch of wild strawberries. It soon become apparent to Joseph that both Jack's and Sadie's appetites were not limited to their customary foods. Time soon passed, and it was time to bring the goats back to the corral.

On the way back to the stables, Joseph decided he would have to rework the saddle blanket; it was not long enough to accommodate the border collie too. *All of a sudden, his clothes made him uncomfortable. What Indian brave would wear these clothes?*

He remembered a bundle packed with clothes that would be just right. Joseph knew he was late for supper, so he gave Sadie an extra ration of feed and a quick rub down and brushed her in the best spots before rushing off to the house.

Jack made his bed next to Sadie's stall and was about to close his eyes when he noticed a cat on the ledge above him. So, this is the elusive one who has avoided revealing itself. *It was not a large cat, the size that the people living in the cities would have.*

Jack wondered how it would survive in the rugged country with all the larger predators around. Maybe it is not really a cat. *It would be the first cat that did not puff up like a possum, and it even smelled okay. He just did not care if the cat was there or not.*

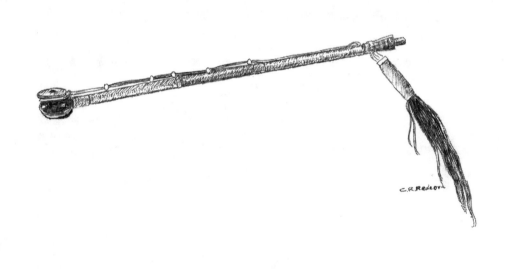

CHAPTER EIGHT:

IMAGERY: "THE SPOKEN LANGUAGE"

Rays of sunlight were just filtering through the mountain peaks as Joseph opened his eyes the next morning. From his window on the second story of the family's ranch house, he could watch the sun emerge over the river and mountains beyond. Still not awake, he began to drift back asleep with images of the river and mountains still in his thoughts.

Not asleep or fully awake, Joseph's visions became both dreamlike and realistic. It was if he were hovering over the river and could see everything all at one time. He could hear his sister's voice telling him not to be nervous—everything would be okay.

As he looked on, an Indian village began to appear on both sides of the river. It became so real that he could see the smoke from the fires and hear sounds of the village. With each new emerging image he felt himself become part of the village. He was being drawn to an older woman standing at the edge of the village. The woman turned and began to wave to him.

The next instant he was in his room wide-awake. Joseph could never remember having a dream like this before. He quickly sat up looked out *the window to see if the Indian village was there. No, but all the same he thought it was so real it must have been there at some time.*

Joseph hurried down to the morning meal, trying to block the dream out of his memory. He had just sat down to eat as his twin sister entered the room. This morning she was dressed just like the woman in his dream. Seeing his concern, Ida Belle explained that it was the dress given to her by Warmwind many years ago. She was now grown up enough to wear it.

Joseph could tell from the sound of her voice that she knew of the dream he had experienced. He also noticed her eyes sparkle when he recognized the dress. If he had to be a twin, he would have liked to have a brother instead of a sister. He would never understand girls.

Ida Belle not only understood her brother but believed their lives were eternally intertwined. She wondered why being twins they were they so different; the ideas and inspirations she experienced must come from a source beyond her. Was he not also someone on whom a mystical power was bestowed?

He did not even acknowledge Warmwind's gift to them this morning. She knew their lives to be so joined with their great-grandmother's and could feel something extraordinary was now going to happen in their lives. If only her brother could understand.

Joseph had other things on his mind as he left the house. Most important, would his dog ride on the back of his Indian pony for a second time? Had the Indian pony been willing to help, allowing the border collie to keep his balance? There were rumors of how cowboys would suddenly lose their balance and plunge into a stream or nose-dive into a thorny brush while riding her.

It was a little strange that she would treat the border collie in such a friendly way. It was all a little confusing for Joseph. Dogs were dogs, horses were horses, and all the mystical stuff was for girls like his sister, and that was that.

He had not noticed the bond that had formed between his two companions. In some twist of fate, they had risen above the confines that the natural world had imposed on their species. Each was unable to accept the monotonous existence they were expected to live. The boy was exciting to be around and had become their escape into another world.

Jack had carried out his morning routine and resumed his watch over the surrounding terrain when the girl once again came out with a biscuit covered with gravy. This time he kept his composure, acknowledged her gift, ate quickly and raced to catch up with the boy. Before long, they were inside the tack room with the boy busily making alteration to his Indian blanket saddle.

Jack noticed that Sadie had come in from the pasture and was looking in a window that opened up into the alleyway. The boy had also noticed but was not paying much attention to her. Just as Jack placed one of his paws on the boy's leg, Sadie gave out an impatient moan.

Wondering what would be next, the boy opened the window and returned to his task. Sadie waited patiently as the boy tried out his latest strategy. She preferred the first blanket but thought this one would have additional possibilities this winter.

At last, the boy was ready to take the goats to pasture. Both Sadie and Jack were anxious to begin another day of adventure and to explore the valley. They did not mind helping the boy manage the goats. After the goats were grazing, the boy would only have to ensure the herd's safety until it was time to bring them back to the corral. What could go wrong with the two Great Pyrenees watching over them?

When they reached the goat corral Jack could tell something was not right. Both the Great Pyrenees were standing outside the herd. Still the boy opened the gate and sent him in to head the goats to pasture. Jack was still feeling a little bit uneasy as the boy signaled him toward a valley between *two mountain ridges. His fears diminished some, as the two Great Pyrenees also understood the boy's commands and led the way.*

Once they reached the valley, Jack scouted the valley parameters just to make sure it was okay. Still there was something there he could not put out of his subconscious. He could tell the two Great Pyrenees were also uneasy with the circumstances. At last, the goats were grazing and the Great Pyrenees had taken up their watch. He could do no more.

Joseph had selected this valley because of the grass and a water basin, but it also led up onto a mountain peak. Here he could explore the mountain and still watch the goat herd. Joseph relaxed as his Indian pony made her way up the mountainside. Once on the mountain peak he scanned the valley, making sure the goats were okay.

The three companions were soon uncovering every detail of the mountain ridge. The boy looked for a present for his sister, the border collie chased down smells he had never experienced, and the Indian pony found sweet tasting forage to eat. Joseph had just found an amethyst stone that appeared to have changed color when the border collie gave out an abrupt alarm.

From the mountain peak, Joseph could see the goat herd in a panic. The two Great Pyrenees were not in sight. He quickly mounted his Indian pony without the mouthpiece. He had found out she would respond with his movements just as well.

Down the mountainside the three companions raced, only to find a family of skunks defending their burrow. Jack, not wanting any further trouble, did his best to apologize to the family of skunks, keeping his distance.

The two Great Pyrenees sat nearby, obviously not happy with the whole incident. It became clear that three teenage billy goats had instigated the crisis. The smell was unavoidable. Jack and the Great Pyrenees could sense something else was behind the disturbance. Neither one could remember these three goats being in the goat heard before.

Following the boy's commands, Jack soon had the goat herd headed back to the corrals. It was a slow procession. While Sadie, the Great Pyrenees, and the rest of the goat herd tried to keep a distance from the three teenagers, Jack managed to keep them all aimed at the corrals. Upon reaching the corral, the three troublemakers were immediately placed in solitary confinement.

Sadie had noticed that Jack was tired after working so hard. To the boy's amazement Jack easily leaped onto Sadie's back, and with care, the three companions returned to the stables. It was a good time for Sadie; after work she could roam the small pasture that opened out from her stall, and she could always count on Jack keeping her company between his rounds about the ranch compound.

After completing his chores, Joseph began searching the tack room for a box to hold the seven-sided amethyst stone he had found for his sister's birthday gift. He remembered there was a small basket on the shelf where he had found great-grandmother's basket.

It was perfect, Joseph thought; the amethyst stone fit into the miniature basket as if it was made just for it. He placed the stone into the basket and decided he would place it on his sister's bed when he heard her coming into the stables.

Before Joseph could hide her present, Ida Belle said, "Joseph, Joseph, Warmwind is here." Joseph tried to listen to everything his sister was telling him. Most of what she was saying did not make much sense, and the rest was not important to him until she said "Joseph what do you have for me."

Joseph thought, How could she possible know about the present? *It was impossible to surprise her. He might as well give it to her now. To his surprise, after opening the basket, she gave out a penetrating shriek and raced out of the stables holding the basket out in front of her. He was sure he would never understand his sister or any other girl either.*

Ida Belle had instantaneously connected with the amethyst stone. The image of a large cat had emerged on one face of the stone. She had closed the basket cover and raced to her room trying to decide what to do. Once in her room, she regained her composure and opened the cover. As she looked into the basket, the dark blue stone began to change color, becoming dark green.

After some thought Ida Belle picked up the stone to examine more closely; there were seven different surfaces, each conveying a different significance to her. Again, the image of a large, dark green-colored cat began to appear on one face. Ida Belle decided she would go to her great-grandmother for counsel.

It was time for supper when Joseph could no longer find anything to keep him busy at the horse stables. His border collie and Indian pony had both come into the stables after hearing his sisters shriek. He would never want to give up his two companions, but his life was so much simpler a few days ago.

Sure, there was good and bad. And maybe his sister had good reasons to act the way she did. He was fourteen now and expected to do his share of the work and responsibilities. It did not make any sense to play around with mystical nonsense. Possibly that was the reason he was putting off seeing his great-grandmother.

Reluctantly Joseph made his way to the house and up the stairs to his great-grandmother's room. The door was open, so he called, "Warmwind."

From inside the room a faint voice answered, "Joseph, is that you? What has taken you so long to come see me?"

Upon entering the room, Joseph found his great-grandmother sitting on a multicolored rug. He sat down beside her, asking, "Favored Grandmother can I bring in a chair for you? We have rocking chairs that would be more comfortable."

Warmwind thanked him and then replied, "Sometimes life should not be comfortable It is better if I am not comfortable, at least until I have finished all that I must."

Joseph thought she was just as confusing as his sister was. What could she possible have to do at her age?

Then Joseph asked if she would like to have help going downstairs to dinner. She replied, "Your sister has provided me with all the nourishment I require."

Okay, whatever that means, *Joseph thought as he left the room.*

At the evening meal, there was talk of Warmwind and of the war. Joseph noticed Ida Belle had moved from her normal place and was sitting beside him. His thoughts changed when his father asked about the goat herd and said to Jack, "What happen today with the goats?

The border collie sure was working hard to bring them in."

Joseph, knowing it was not going to turn out good, began by saying, "There was this den of skunks." He would say no more with all the laughter around the table.

Seeing his discomfort, the others turned the conversation to the cattle herd. He should be on the lookout for stray cattle as his older brothers were bringing the cattle herd east of the Little Piney Creek. There could be problems from predators and with enraged cows since it was calving time.

The conversation changed to a fair and rodeo that was going to be at the end of the summer. The main interest for the family was a cutting horse event. There was a disagreement over which of the horses would be the best.

Joseph knew there would no need for him to be involved. Before he left the table, Ida Belle, without looking at him, whispered, "Joseph, Warmwind would like us to visit her tonight after dinner Please come as soon as you can."

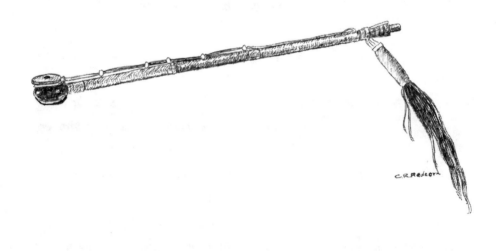

Chapter Nine:

An intriguing mystery

Sarah's closed the journal; it was old and badly worn. Was the journal really written in the year 1916? Who wrote it, and why was it written in both English and French? Yes, she had taken French as a second language, but the journal could not have been written just for her.

"Who were Ida Belle and Joseph?" She whispered. "Who wrote the journals, and when were they written?"

To Sarah's disbelief, behind her came the soft voice of Hanna, answering, "Joseph would be your great-grandfather, and Ida Belle would be his twin sister."

Hanna continued. "About who wrote the journal I cannot say. By the way, Misty thinks please do not be offended, but maybe you can start ridding without a saddle, and she feels much better without the bridle."

Sarah started to say, "Where did you come from, Hanna?", but instead one stirring question raced through her mind.

If Joseph was my great-grandfather and he did not believe in such things as an invisible world and in spirits why should I? If it were true the journal would have been written when he was fourteen—that would have been 1916. It is possible.

Then probably whoever wrote the journal could have been part of the family. It could have been Ida Belle. No, not Ida Belle, she thought, remembering how the journal started: "It is the occasion of their fourteenth year." The one who wrote the journal was writing about Joseph and Ida Belle.

Sarah regained her composure and asked Hanna, "What else does Misty think about the way I ride?"

Hanna brought her horse alongside of Misty, saying, "Please understand, it is not like that." Trying not to say more, she asked, "Did you get to meet Quinton"?

"Yes," Sarah answered. "It was all very strange the way his dog showed up and led me to an isolated valley where I met Quinton. The animals, they seem to be acting on their own. Quinton, he was surprised to see me. Why are you smiling?"

Hanna could not control her laughter, saying, "Do not be cross; it is a special gift."

"Oh," Sarah responded, thinking, I, like Joseph in the journal, will not let myself go there; it just a natural occurrence, Hanna too, not a special gift of some kind. Sarah was determined to discover more about the invisible influence that seemed to surround the family.

Sarah found herself even more skeptical. There was no doubt in her mind that Joseph would be her great-grandfather and that the ranch in the journal was the same one she was on today. It was all a little too ordered almost planned—but by who and why?

"You must excuse me," Hanna cried out. "It is getting late, and I am needed to help with the evening meal."

Sarah called back as Hanna rode off, "If you leave your horse in the stables I will take care of her for you." Sarah watched Hanna until she was out of sight; she trusted her more than anyone, but she needed time alone to think.

When Sarah reached the stables her grandfather had led Hanna's horse into the stalls and was pitching hay from the hayloft. "I missed you," he called to her. "You must not be amused with me; I have not taken care of horses for a long time now."

"I have missed you, too," Sarah responded. "I am glad you are here; I have a lot to tell you. You look quite at home up there."

"So this is the notorious Misty," he said, climbing down the ladder, "Cousin John said she was a descendent of a horse my father took care of when he was about your age. We can talk while we work with the horses if you like."

Sarah fed a scoop of grain to Misty, carefully considering what she would say to her grandfather. She did not want to sound foolish or even worse for him to believe she had been taken in by her cousins.

"Grandfather, would you think I was being foolish if I was imagining there is a mysterious invisible influence that surrounds our family and this ranch? The journal I have been reading, I believe it is about great-grandfather and his sister, Ida Belle, when they were fourteen."

"Of course not," he answered. "Tell me more about the journal; Cousin John said no one had been able to interpret the letters and symbols. How did you manage to figure it out?"

"I could not on my own; together with Hanna we were able to figure it out. Hanna was able to tell me about the symbols, and when I realized the letters were spelling a mixture of English and French words, it came easy. I still do not understand why it is so easy to read.

"The haunted house, Hanna, Quinton, the journal—it is all a little bit too prearranged, almost designed; I don't know who or why. That is what I wanted to talk to you about. In the journal it was written Ida

Belle's sacred basket was only to be handed down to the next gifted one.

"Why did Cousin John give the journal and the sacred basket to Hanna, and I and why did he tell us everything has changed now that we have come to the ranch? It may have been obvious to him, but it was not obvious to me.

"There is something else. The scenes that you drew in your workshop of Native American Indian life while I was there with you—they are all here in the special room. Not the same ones—these are very old and must have been drawn many years ago, but even so they are alike in every detail."

"It is a mystery," he murmured. "I wish I had the answer." How he could tell her of his dream and that the answer he was certain only she could discover? "I believe we will find the answer, but right now we will have to go to supper."

By midmorning the next day Sarah and Hanna had once more returned to the river and their out-of-the-way hideaway. As Sarah begin to read once more, she could not get Hanna out of her mind—not that she was that much different from herself; it was an unexplainable charisma that seemed to be about her. It was almost the same as that she experienced around her grandfather.

Unable to continue, she asked Hanna if she would like to read the journal this time. Hanna only answered, "If you would like."

Sarah had to say, "Tell me what you are saying."

Hanna could only answer, "Please, you must understand, in my grandmother's home it was not only the words spoken; it was in the sound, and within the silence between words, that she would communicate with to me. It is not in the words you are reading but in your voice that the real meaning of the journal is made known to me."

Okay, Sarah thought, I am just thankful you are here with me; my grandfather was right too. Hesitating for a moment, Sarah considered what Hanna had just said; it was not in the words I was reading but in my voice.

Another mystery: I am in some unexplainable way able to understand and read the journal; and from the variations or something within my voice she hears a different meaning that is true. How do I know the real meaning, where does it come from? Sarah began to read once more, this time trying to listen to her voice as well.

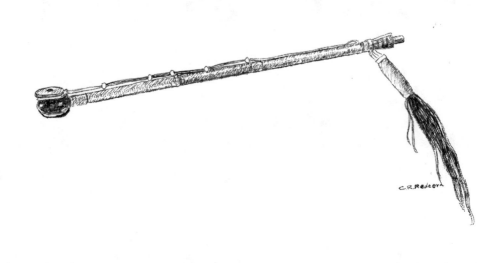

Part Three:

THE ENDOWMENT

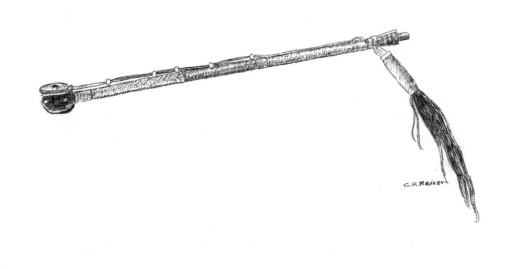

Chapter Ten:

Inherent nature

Joseph's first thoughts were he would see if the rumors about his great-grandmother were true. He could always find something that would require his attention where he would not be able to stay long. It was a good plan; his father had warned him about predators. He could not stay long and would have to leave early to make preparations for the next day.

However, as he walked up the stairs, he began to remember his father telling him his great-grandmother had met Chief Blackdog and many of the other great chiefs. Maybe even Chief Shunkahmolah; that would be all right, and he would stay longer. He could always suddenly recall the need for him to leave.

Ida Belle was already in their great-grandmother's room when Joseph came in. It was difficult for Joseph to keep from smiling when he found his great-grandmother in one of their best rocking chairs. Nevertheless, he was pleased to see her more comfortable.

He was sure Ida Belle had influenced her in some way to sit in the rocking chair. He really was proud of his sister's ability to strengthen and encourage everyone around her. She had a way of knowing just what to say or do. He was about to sit down beside Ida Belle when Warmwind begin to talk.

Raising her eyes to Joseph, Warmwind spoke first in a way that he had not experienced before; then, seeing his amazement, she said, "You must not mind my old-fashioned ways. Our Native Indian speech is quite different than that which you are speaking today; the imagery that is of our speech conveys a different meaning to the mind."

Warmwind, knowing what she was saying was new to Joseph but not to Ida Belle, leaned back in her rocking chair, allowing her young great-grandson to comprehend what she had revealed to him.

Ida Belle did understand everything her great-grandmother had said and more. She did not flinch or look away when their eyes met, and the knowledge of the centuries passed between them.

Joseph thought the rumors about his great-grandmother were true but not the way he had heard them. She was a little old fashioned, well very old fashioned, but was not crazy or unnatural. She made a lot of sense; he had often thought of most things in a different way than others.

Well, maybe it is somewhat in the same way Ida Belle thinks too. *If he translated what he read or heard into his own thoughts, let it sort of drift around, different images would emerge in his mind. In a way it was just as his great-grandmother had said.*

His thoughts were interrupted as Ida Belle asked her great-grandmother about the visions. First the one Joseph had encountered in the mountains and of the chant he had sung there; secondly of their dream of the village and of the girl that waved to Joseph. "This is most disturbing," she said. "I do not know the meaning of such things. Will you tell us what it is all about?"

Warmwind begin rocking in her chair; how could she trust her perception and thoughts into such affairs, especially now at her age? Nevertheless, she must do something to help her two young great-grandchildren. She realized her great-grandchildren looked upon nature and all its natural forms from a different perspective and drew from them different meaning than those of her generation.

With a sigh, she said, "It is not for this one to give meaning to the visions that have been made known to you. You must understand such knowledge is a gift and cannot be perceived by others. I can only tell you of such experiences I have known and that of such occurrences passed down from your ancestors."

She continued, "On the occasion of my fifteenth year our clan chose to leave our council lodge and move to a more desirable land. One member of the clan, Whitedeer, vanished along with our clan's sacred objects handed down through the generation. We searched many days throughout the mountains and valleys, but there was not a trace of her.

"Many years later, at the time of her death, she visited me in a dream. She spoke to me from the entrance to a cavern surrounded by high cliffs that opened to the sky. In the dream the voices of many generations became one, and the spirits awakened the otherworld. On the sides of the rock walls faded figures and symbols summoned me to come to them. I could not.

"You must find the cavern and learn what I could not, for now I am too old and long for the time when I will journey into the world of spirits and join my ancestors."

Ida Belle asked, "How can we find this place? We know not of Whitedeer, of the hidden cavern, or of the clan's sacred objects."

Warmwind said, "It is as you say—if you would like we will talk of such things."

Joseph thought, This is all very foolish—now she is speaking nonsense. *While that kind of talk by women was to be expected, was he to become an accomplice in such things? Sure there are some things that are hard to explain. Should he start imagining spirits in his dreams or a mischievous one playing tricks on him?*

No, it all can all be explained; what is the difference between that man Nostradamus, who lived in the sixteenth century, and Ida Belle. He must have had supernatural powers, which enabled him to know the future. Ida

Belle sure has. His great-grandmother was old; she had a right to imagine anything she wanted. If she wants us to find out what happen to Whitedeer and learn about our ancestors, what will it hurt? It might be interesting.

For Ida Belle it was very clear: the thoughts and images that had emerged from the shadows of her mind since she could first remember were now very real. The spirits of the ancestors had visited her in dreams as long as she could remember.

With a quick glance toward her brother, Ida Belle thanked her great-grandmother for the gift she had given them this morning. To her surprise, Warmwind said she did not know of any gift she had given to them.

Warmwind only smiled and continued, "Our ancestors did not practice the art of writing; it was within the form of rituals that the most treasured of our learning and history was recorded for all time. As you have heard me say, we had little need for words and did not have a written language. The rituals became the vessel by which our ancestors passed down from one generation to the next that which they held most sacred.

"There were others, the makers of images, they could make maps, draw pictures that tell of events, and tell a story by symbols and pictures. There came a time when our leaders no longer communicated the meaning of our ancestors.

"And then there were others living in two worlds—the world as you know it to be and in the shadows of an invisible world—who found favor with the Great Spirit Wakonda gaining much knowledge and insight." After a deep sigh her voice faded away while she was saying something about the maker of images.

It seemed to take forever before his great-grandmother would speak again. Ida Belle touched Joseph on the shoulder and told him Warmwind had drifted off to sleep. They would have to leave now. She did not tell him of the conversation she had with her great-grandmother earlier that day.

Chapter Eleven:

The nature of courage

Joseph had difficulty sleeping that night. His mind kept going back over all that had happened that day. What puzzled him the most was how quickly his life had changed. Up until a few days ago, he felt in complete control of his life.

Finally, he decided to just not pay any attention to any outside distractions and to return to his carefree life. It would be okay to visit with Warmwind at night and listen to her stories. All of the mystical stuff he would ignore. He soon fell asleep.

Joseph woke to the smell of his mother cooking the morning meal. When he entered the kitchen there was talk of the work planned for the day. He smiled and began to relax as the conservation turned to the weather. His father thought it best to move the goat herd east of Little Piney Creek and into the northeast ridge.

To his relief, there was not any talk of Warmwind. Life was back to normal. As he finished eating his mother reminded him to take the leather pack containing his noonday meal. Ida Belle was quick to bring the pack to him. Joseph wondered what she is up to now as he caught that sparkle in her eyes.

Before long, the three companions were moving the goat herd from the corral and into the valley of the eastern mountain ridges. Joseph had explored the valley many times before. He had often wanted to follow a trail that led up into the mountains to a place called Moccasin Gap.

The trail had once been a path many animals followed crossing the mountains. Later Native Americans of many nations used it. It became a trail as others came into the mountains. There was talk of making it a road for wagons to cross the mountains. He hoped not; that would spoil the mountain forever.

Once the goats were grazing in the valley, Jack led the way as they traveled up the trail to Moccasin Gap. He was careful not to let the boy out of his sight. He soon found out the trail followed a zigzag pattern around the mountain edges. So that is it. *Jack now knew there were many mountains running in the zigzag collection of ridges. At one point, he could look out over the ranch and see that the main valley branched off into many smaller valleys nestled between the mountain ridges.*

Joseph could tell the border collie was not going very far from him. It was the first time the border collie kept such a close watch on him. Farther up the mountain, Joseph dismounted and walked ahead of his Indian pony. The sides of the mountains were steep and slippery. Once they reached the mountain breach, they could see both sides of the mountain range. Far off Joseph thought he could see the Buffalo River.

As Joseph set down to eat his midday meal, both Jack and Sadie came up beside him. Joseph laughed, saying, "You must speak to me if I am to listen to your voice." His laughter was met with an equal vocal response from his impenitent companions. As he opened his pack, he understood. In the pack, there were dried beef strips and bread cakes for him. There was also a sweet cake with bacon for the border collie and carrots for his pony.

There was not any doubt why the border collie had not let him out of his sight all morning. Jack could smell the piece of sweet cake and bacon in the leather pack. He never took his eyes off the boy or the pack for very long. And, yes, he did listen to the assertions within the laughter of the boy, and that was to be expected from such a human.

As the three explorers came out from the mountain trail, the goats were nowhere to be seen. Joseph scanned the valley below to see the goats had wandered down by Little Piney Creek. He gave the border collie the command to herd the goats and motioned for him to circle around them.

Joseph could see a billy goat escaping into a thicket. He motion for the border collie to go after the other goats as he dismounted and went into the thickets to get the goat.

He was searching for the billy goat when he stumbled onto a newborn calf. The calf cried out, and the mother cow came charging toward him. Joseph could hear her crashing through the brush as he ran for a large tree.

Suddenly there was a bigger crash and then silence. Joseph turned to see the cow getting up from the ground. The border collie was in a stalking stance between him and the cow. Both the boy and his dog quickly retreated from the thicket to see the billy goat and the rest of the herd frantically running wild around the valley.

Joseph first hugged his dog and then examined his dog, finding one of his front legs had been bruised when he threw the cow to the ground. Still the border collie would not quit his job and began to move the goat herd back to the goat corral. To Joseph's surprise, Sadie began to help her companion herd the goats.

At first, the goats were too quick for Joseph to stay on Sadie's back without almost falling off. After a little while Joseph was easily keeping his balance and Sadie was outmaneuvering the goats. By the time they reached the goat corral the trio was a team. This time as they returned to the stables, the border collie rode on Joseph's lap, while the Indian pony was careful not to falter.

Joseph had never considered before what life was all about; oh, he did think about his family and others but not about all living things as being part of one life form. The dog had saved him from the angry cow, and then together with the horse had they acted with one single purpose. It was expected of a family, singleness of purpose, but not of animals too. He had never thought of animals as being courageous either, but Jack sure was.

When they reached the stables Ida Belle was there waiting for them. In her hands, she carried a small bottle of wild valerium. The border collie followed her into the stables, where two drops of the herb was added to his drinking water. In a very short time after drinking the herbal medicine, the border collie had recovered.

Earlier that day Ida Belle and her great-grandmother had spent the morning going over herbs to treat diseases and other ailments. This afternoon she had searched around Little Piney Creek for herbs. The wild valerium had special importance for her.

The evening meal passed without much significance for Joseph. His sister again had left her place across the table to sit beside him. He let his older brothers know of the cow and calf down at Little Piney Creek. He left out the part about the cow charging him, knowing his mother and father would worry about him. Ida Belle immediately understood his motives, giving her understanding approval as she gently clear her throat and left the table.

Warmwind sat slowly rocking back and forth in her rocking chair as she tried to focus her thoughts on what she must say next to the twins. As a young girl, she had listened to the old ones talk with such pride of their people and their way of life.

For her, it had been a constant struggle, forced to bend to the demands of a changing world. How could she tell them of such pain and suffering during her lifetime? No! She would tell them of how their ancestors remained courageous and honorable, with a good deal of humility.

While waiting for the twins it suddenly became very important for her to remember the very first time she was actually happy. She closed her eyes to let her mind concentrate. Yes. She could remember. She was twelve years old when the clan had traveled over the mountains into the valley of peace. Like in a dream world she was twelve again, relieving her first adventure into the valley of the vapors.

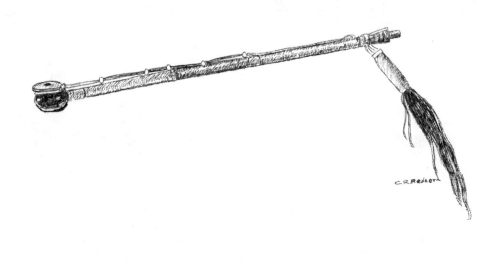

CHAPTER TWELVE:

THE INVISIBLE WORLD AND SPIRITS

Warmwind often asked herself why had she lived so long and was it so important that she discover what had happened to Whitedeer. New generations would surely leave behind many traditions of her clan as her generation had done so many years ago. Even now, was not the Great Spirit that created the universe guiding the ones that were to follow into a new age of living?

Where are the modern storytellers and gifted ones of today! She was confident the Great Spirit would guide her as she counseled the twins and in some way those who would come after. It was the mystery of the invisible world and elusive spirits that she found so hard to speak of.

A warm summer rain had settled over the valley, allowing the twins to have a day away from their normal activities. A little after lunch they had both found their way into Warmwind's room. After asking about their school and what was happening around the ranch, Warmwind asked, "Where you would like me to begin today?"

Ida Belle quickly said, "Tell us first about storytellers and of the gifted ones."

"No." Joseph shook his head, thinking about Jack and Sadie. "Tell us about the warriors and how the animals helped them." With a sigh Warmwind understood what was unspoken; what they really wanted to ask about was of the mysterious spirits and of an invisible universe that now was only mentioned of as a former time.

"Yes, the storytellers, gifted ones, and spirits." Warmwind nodded her head. "It is where we should begin. It would be impossible to tell you about them unless you know how the ancient Native American Indians thought about themselves and of the visible and invisible universe the Great Spirit Wakonda had created for all living creatures.

"They considered themselves no better or worse than any other living species that they encountered. It was a wonderful time as they shared the land, the rivers, and nature with the birds, reptiles, and animals. They believed the spirit of Wakonda was within all things.

"Although as far as strength, cunning, and natural intelligence they accepted the superiority of other species, they were determined to develop basic skills to survive and strengthen themselves. They were humbled by the talents and experience Wakonda had bestowed on other species.

"They made every effort to learn from them the proper behavior and to take their place in the natural order of life. It was not always agreed upon which of Wakonda creations that best possessed the wisdom of the universe, and they disagreed on which ones they should model their behavior after.

"Should it be a bird for their eyesight, the bear for their sense of smell, or the elk because of their hearing? Still others thought it should be that of a gentle wind or the starlit night sky."

Joseph, thinking he knew the answer, asked. "Are you talking about totems?"

"Yes," Warmwind answered, "It is something like totems and the most likely reason why the ancients organized themselves into tribes and clans, each preferring their own totem. The tribe members celebrated the power

of their totem and taught their children to follow in the same behavior as they observed in their totem.

"It was more than a preference of one species or natural occurrence over another; the survival through the winter could depend on how well a clan could read the signs displayed by the birds, reptiles, and animals. By reading the signs correctly the tribe could foresee impending harsh weather, locate superior hunting grounds, learn new medicines, and acquire other skills to enrich their lives. It was a matter of recognizing the spiritual powers within all things."

Ida Belle glanced at her brother in a knowing way, causing him to ask his great-grandmother were the legends true where after departing this life some of the old ones took the shape of a bird or animal? Warmwind could see the difference of opinion between her two great grandchildren and thought she should not answer his question directly.

"It is not for me to say; it is the belief of almost all Native American Indians that the natural order of the universe is one of balance. The plants, birds, and animals are all beings equal to humans—like a forest that would not be a forest without the rain, air, sun, wind, and even the fires each keeping the balance. The stories you speak of are about that balance in nature, where the presence of Wakonda is everywhere and in all beings."

Ida Belle said, "It is of the spirit you speak."

Warmwind nodded her head and said, "During a great tragedy or illness it was thought that balance was lost or disrupted. To regain that balance, prayer and ceremonies were performed by the spiritual leaders, imploring all beings to restore the balance. You can see that in spirit, animals could become humans or humans could become animals. Not all, of course, only the gifted.

"Those who processed such superior skills were revered by the clans and elevated to a high position. That person, a gifted one, as you have asked about, was recognized by the clan as an authority on the spirits, the other

worlds, and medicines and would intercede with Wakonda in matters of the clan. Their bond with nature and other forms of life set them apart from the rest of the clan."

Joseph politely interrupted Warmwind, saying, "Okay, the gifted ones were great, but do the animals know there is a great spirit, and is there more than one spirit?"

Ida Belle spoke out, saying, "Gifted ones have always been part of our people, bringing about balance and harmony."

Warmwind only smiled and said, "It may be best if we talk later of the gifted ones.

"I have told you of the storytellers that recited stories, spoke of current events, and passed on legends of our tribe. The storytellers said the animals knew a mischievous spirit, the trickster, very well. There were many tales of the trickster using the animals and people for their amusement. The storytellers were held in a high regard by the people of the villages for keeping their tribal history alive.

"There were storytellers of our tribe that spoke of the sky people who lived in the heavens way beyond the earth. Wakonda, the creative force of the universe, sent them to the surface of the earth, where they joined the earth people to form the Niukonska nation. Those who came after were called 'People of the Middle Waters.'

"There were also other storytellers that told of people who lived in the sky way beyond the earth. They were the children of their father the sun and their mother the moon. Their mother sent them to live on the earth. Finding the earth covered with water, they asked for help from the birds and animals. The elk called to the wind to blow away the water from the earth, causing the soil to produce beans, corn, grasses, and trees.

"No one knows if that is true. Our storytellers would only say the 'children of the middle waters' was the beginning of our tribe. Still, our native language was that of the Siouan Nation, which may tell something *of our heritage. Who the sky people were and where they came from may have been disclosed in the sacred object lost with Whitedeer. I don't know for sure.*

"In their early days we know the Niukonska villages were separated into two groups called the Sky People and the Earth People; it is possible that Siouan Indian's 'the earth people' joined with an unknown people 'the sky people' to form the Wazhazhe nation. And that was when our forefathers may have first begun to turn away from the ways of the natural world.

"Later the people of Wazhazhe nation settled along the Osage River in western Missouri, where they lived by a set of laws and traditions established by a group of elders known as the 'Little Old Men.' To become one of 'the little old men' young boys slight in stature but gifted with exceptional cleverness passed through seven stages of learning.

"There was less need of gifted ones, and the storytellers would tell more about the heroic acts of the tribe rather than of wonders of other species they once respected and imitated. Still, the clans held on to some of their traditional and honored their totems in ceremonies."

Warmwind could see both Joseph and Ida Belle were becoming uncomfortable. She paused for a moment and said, "I would like to tell you more later about the Europeans, the Indian wars, the treaties, and the reservations; for now I must rest."

Ida Belle and Joseph left her room, each absorbed in their own thoughts. Their great-grandmother had talked much about the world of spirits; it must be their native Indian ancestors believed spirits were part of their world. Warmwind was right they were disturbed, but not by what she had been saying alone.

Not living on the reservation, they had to attend the government school, and there were many things they had not considered before. Joseph had to search for stories and information about his heritage on his own, and that was okay. He was free to study in his own way. But most of the time he had to learn all about the Europeans, and that had been an inconvenience for him, except for one man: an Italian named Michelangelo.

The teacher had talked of his paintings and of his architecture designs. That was not what Joseph had found interesting. Michelangelo grew up on a farm like him and went on to design many weapons for war. It struck him Michelangelo would have probably been one of the little old men if he had lived in the Wazhazhe nation.

Jack had been waiting for Joseph to come out of the house from his special advantage spot. He watched the boy as he walked to the stables. For a moment, he concentrated on the room where the girl now stayed. He could feel her anxiety. He was now drawn to both the girl and the boy.

It was a matter of who needed him the most. To that, he looked at the house once more and then followed the boy into the stables. Joseph spent the rest of the day designing a rope and pulley for the window that opened into the tack room so Sadie could open the window herself.

Sadie had watched Joseph as he worked and learned that when she pulled on the rope the window would open. Joseph was satisfied and assumed he would not be bothered opening the window again. He had forgotten that sometimes he might have wanted to have some privacy.

The next morning Sadie had noticed the change in her two friends; still, life was short, and she planned to make the best of it. Twice she had to take charge of the job at hand when the goats were moved to forage above the ranch house.

At the edge of the mountain, a rock formation extended out into the valley. On one side of the rock formation woodlands expanded from the mountains down into the valley. On the other side a grassy slope spanned down the hill to the stables below.

It was her first time in this part of the ranch. She chose this area because earlier that morning she could see a new place to explore. It was a lazy day for the three friends. After searching the rock formations for traces of ancient

Indian artifacts, Joseph stretched out on the grassy slope thinking about what life must have been for his ancestors.

Jack had searched the rock formations along with the boy. This was copperhead snake country. He could smell the venomous snakes from a distance off. The smell of the rocks contaminated by the snakes dulled his senses. After a while, he gave in to the warm sun and lay down beside Joseph on the soft grass. Soon both were soundly sleeping.

It was late in the afternoon when Sadie was ready to return to the stables. Joseph woke up to the touch of a soft muzzle nudging him and the smell of strong wild onion breath. His complaints to Sadie only brought more nuzzling and a whinny that could only be from pleasure.

He shook his head and tried to focus on the rock formation and the trees beyond. What he was seeing was not at all right. The goat herd was in the trees, jumping off a nearby ridge, or just standing like statues.

Jack became on the alert as Joseph jumped to his feet; both raced down to find out what was going on. The Great Pyrenees was frantically trying to find and confront an invisible perpetrator.

Jack began by moving as much of the herd as possible into the open grasslands. Just as soon as the boy removed a goat from the trees or rocks, he drove it to the others. Finally, the last three troublesome goats were all that were missing. Jack was sure they were the same ones that harassed the skunk and her family before.

Out of a stand of large weeds and flowers three goats staggered with dazed eyes, chewing on green weed stems. Joseph knew immediately the goat herd had been eating locoweed. Occasionally, a horse or cow would mistake locoweed and eat it. However, not a whole herd. Goats must be the dumbest of all.

Joseph began to laugh as he remembered one billy goat that kept charging the trunk of a tree. Jack was not satisfied as he drove the goat herd down the grassy slope and into the goat corral. He was not sure if the trickster was behind the problem.

The Pyrenees were still a mystery to him. Their intelligence would be the equal of his in some ways. It must be their only concern was the protection of the goat herd or they would recognize their predicament. From now on, he would have to watch the three teenage goats more closely.

After returning to the stables, Jack and Sadie watched Joseph as he searched through the drawers containing old and obsolete tools. They could see no benefit in the strange hammer and wood chisels he was so pleased to remember.

They were even more puzzled when he brought a wooden post into the tack room and began cutting off pieces. Each was curious to what he was doing. The boy had notched five lines around the post, each an equal distance apart. On one side of the top space he began to chip it into a figure that resembled a bear. Sadie lost interest, deeming his efforts of little value, but Jack was not so sure.

Later at the evening meal, Joseph reported the locoweed to his father and brothers. After much discussion of the matter, a plan to avoid the area was arranged. All agreed Joseph had handled the problem very well. Still, Joseph knew everyone was glad it was not they who were assigned to the goat herd.

He did not mind; he had time to be with his dog and horse, and he had not forgotten the narrow escape with the cow and her calf. What were becoming more important to him were his evenings with his great-grandmother and finding out what happened to Whitedeer, whoever she was.

Chapter Thirteen:

The council lodge

That next evening the twins found Warmwind sitting on the large rug with a smaller blanket covering her head. She asked the twins to sit in on either side of her facing each other. She informed them that this is how she would like to sit each night.

She then folded the blanket back over her shoulders. Joseph thought it a little strange, but so was everything else these days. Ida Belle was sure it was a way Warmwind could recall the past.

Warmwind began by asking about the ranch and all the animals. She requested that in the evenings would they tell her of the ranch, the animals, and what they experienced that day. Each day Warmwind had watched from her window as her family went about their daily activities.Ida Belle said she would.

Warmwind was about to begin speaking when Joseph asked, "Great-grandmother how is it that you are able to talk in English so well? When you were our age there were no English schools for you to attend."

She replied, "There were not any English schools. That is right, but my sister went to an English school; I learned English and French from her. Now I must return to the history of our ancestors."

Joseph interrupted, saying, "Tell us about Chief Blackdog. Was he not the same age as you?"

"No," Warmwind replied, "he was much older, fifteen years I believe, and I promise I will tell you of all the great leaders later.

"It is important that I tell you most of the knowledge of our ancestors was lost as the storytellers became enchanted with the foreign explorers almost four hundred year ago. The storytellers say the first European to enter the Wazhazhe nation's territory was a Spanish explorer. There is not much to tell except it was the first time warriors and hunters encountered horses.

"With horses the hunters extended their hunting grounds and traveled farther to search for game. With horses the villages did not have to move as much and were built in a more permanent way that included farming."

Joseph said he had read about him, Francisco de Coronado, that was when the goats were first brought to the plains along with the horses. It was okay to bring the horses, but he could have left the goats back in Europe.

Ida Belle thought, Is that all he thinks of?

"After that the French explorers came to many native Indian villages; they were followed by missionaries, traders, and trappers. It was an exciting time as trade with the French brought wealth and prosperity.

"An alliance with France was good, but it alienated some of the Wazhazhe people from their past and with other Indian tribes. The storytellers' narrations had sometimes become misleading and included part of legends and accounts they had heard from the Europeans. Their totems no longer were of the animals and nature that had guided their lives. It was difficult for the people of the villages to know what was true.

"The adjustment was even greater for the gifted ones of old who had always lived their lives learning the wisdoms of nature energies, sharing their knowledge openly with others. Only those with great conviction journeyed

on in the shadows of the everyday world, sharing their wisdom sacredly while marking the way for other to follow.

"The French easily fit in to the Wazhazhe communities north along the Osage River. Without any difficulty they recognized the two divisions: the sky people and the earth people. Each division was made up of family groups you know as clans. The clans had their own site in the village. They chose their own leader to attend the village council lodges and decide on two leaders, one from each division that governed the village.

"Our clan lived farther south, near the Washita mountain range along the White River where the black bears were plentiful. There were other small Wazhazhe villages living in the Arkansas, each of different clan. The French traders only visited our village to buy pelts and furs. It was always a special occasion; a day of celebration when we traded for the European goods.

"Unlike the villages in the north our village did not have a council Lodge. We traveled over the Washita Mountains to a council lodge where the village leaders met and ceremonies were preformed. Each clan had specialized duties that in combination with the other clans served the overall well-being of the tribe. There was a cave just below the council lodge where the clan's sacred bundles were hidden."

Ida Belle said, "Then the legend that the tack room was once a council lodge is true, but why did you say the Washita Mountains?"

Warmwind could see Joseph also did not know and said, "Washita is the Indian word for 'good hunting grounds.' The French spelled it Ouachita, as you know it now. I am surprised a great warrior and hunter such as Joseph did not know that.

"Yes, the tack room was once the council lodge of our clan and others as well. The Spanish came to the Wazhazhe lands some time after the French, not to build an alliance or trade but to preside over all the Indian nations west of the Missouri River. By the year of my birth, the Europeans and the *new nation of the east had gained control over most of the Native American Indian lands."*

Joseph asked, "If our clan left the council lodge to find a better land, why is it in our family today and why did not the Wazhazhe nation let them take over their territory?"

"Yes, it is hard to understand," Warmwind said. "You have to understand the people of the Wazhazhe nation did not believe anyone could own the land or anything else. It was the time of my youth, very difficult." Then a sad expression began to overcome her.

Both Ida Belle and Joseph could see it was a difficult for their great-grandmother to think of that time. With a quick glance they excused themselves and left her room. They knew there was more she was not telling them, and it was not something they would learn about in their school.

Next morning, Ida Belle asked Joseph if he could help her search for plants and herbs. They agreed that Joseph would have a horse saddled and ready for her to ride out to meet him after the noon meal. With all arrangements made Ida Belle quickly finished her morning chores and went to Warmwind's room. This day they would speak of medical plants, minerals, and their intended use.

Joseph, Jack and Sadie were glad to be out in the open air of the wild outdoors again. Joseph had chosen a location that would be safe for the goat herd and close to a stream bound by plants and herbs. The three companions each went off to pursue their own interests, always careful to keep the other two in sight. The strange things that had occurred the last few days had left them nervous and on the lookout.

Joseph found a low, smooth rock formation from which he could watch the goat herd and where Ida Belle would be sure to see him. As he ate his noon meal, he begins to wonder if his great-grandmother would continue telling them about the Europeans or of Indian wars. He could imagine that she would have been something like Ida Belle back then. Like a lightning flash, the image of his great-grandmother's picture in her native dress filled his mind. Joseph quickly dismissed his thoughts and concentrated on the goat herd.

Before long both his dog and his horse were beside him. In the distance, he could see his twin sister riding toward him. He had chosen a smaller, reddish-brown-colored mare for her because it reminded him of his sister. The mare was the most graceful and pleasing of all the stable horses. At that moment, he thought how good it was to have such a sister.

Ida Belle had that same sparkle in her eyes as she greeted Joseph. After a few moments Joseph had to ask, "Is there something the matter?" knowing it must have something to do with him.

Ida Belle replied, "It is only the first time I have seen you in your outdoor clothes." It was then he realized she had never seen him in his leather breeches, moccasins, and a headband before. His sister added, "It would be nice if you would dress this way around the house." Joseph said nothing just leaped onto his Indian pony and started toward the stream and nearby herbs.

Ida Belle rode beside her brother, doing her best to make amends for teasing him. By the time they reached the stream, all had been forgotten and the search for herbs, roots, and minerals began. Jack was quick to clear the area of any snakes while Sadie kept the sorrel horse company. Ida Belle took special care to locate and memorize as many of the plants she could. Today she would only take the plants and herbs suggested by Warmwind.

As they returned to the goat corrals, Ida Belle could feel the eagerness of the horse she was riding to accommodate her every move. She asked if the horse had a name. Her brother shrugged his shoulders, saying, "No one has bothered to give her a name or train her to work with cattle; she is not so strong."

Ida Belle pronounced to her brother, the border collie, and to both horses, that this was to be her horse. She would name her Silver Star because *of the star on her forehead and the silver streaks of hair in her main and tail.*

Back at the stables Joseph set up the stall next to Sadie's for Silver Star. Ida Belle watched her brother feed and brush both horses. When he had finished she said she would braid his hair if he wanted, then raced to the house.

Joseph finished his tasks, changed his clothes, and went back to the house just in time for the evening meal. Ida Belle had moved back to her place across the table from Joseph. She could imagine her brother in real braids, not the way he tied his hair back with leather ties.

After questions about what problem did the goat herd cause today and some laughter the conversation changed to the cattle market and then the war in Europe. What everyone was really concerned with was all how well their chances were to win the cutting horse competition. Joseph decided he would ask how they were doing and if they needed any help.

CHAPTER FOURTEEN:

SPIRITS RACING THROUGH THE SKY

Warmwind had been listening for the footsteps of the twins as they came up the stairs. She could hear that they were walking together and let out a sigh of relief. Even though they would follow different walks of life, their journey would always be as one.

As the twins entered her room she could tell her task would be easier now. Ida Belle was not taking herself so seriously, and Joseph was beginning to become more at ease around her.

Both Ida Belle and Joseph noticed their great-grandmother had that sparkling gleam in her eyes as they sat down on the rug before her. Joseph thought for certain Ida Belle and his great-grandmother were very much alike.

While Ida Belle was telling their great-grandmother about searching for wild plants and herbs, Joseph was wondering what his great-grandmother, like his sister, had in store for him now.

Warmwind said, "To begin, let me tell you of the Wazhazhe nation at the time of my birth. We were the most powerful and creative of all the tribes. We were also great farmers of corn, squash, and other vegetables. But most of all we were a nation of innovation and foresight."

Ida Belle said they were proud of their heritage and of their parents and of their great-grandmother. She gave her great-grandmother an account of their day, especially about Silver Star and the herbs they had found.

Warmwind asked about the other horse Sadie and about the dog Jack.

Joseph had thought often that day about the Europeans and still could not figure out why the Wazhazhe nation did not fight them to keep their territory. He understood all about their belief in not owning the land, but what about giving up their hunting grounds?

He did not want to make his great-grandmother sad again, but it was something he had to know. He would ask her in a way that might not make her sad. Warmwind, seeing Joseph was anxious, said, "Is there anything you would like to talk about?"

Joseph asked, "In all of the books I have read the Wazhazhe nation never went to war with the Europeans; why is that?"

Warmwind said, "It is only difficult to understand because there were not just one reason but there were many. It had to do with the way the Wazhazhe nation thought of themselves.

"They were prosperous and ambitious. Making alliances with the Europeans was their way to advance their culture and to learn new ways. Nevertheless, I must tell you the Spanish did declare war on the Wazhazhe nation.

"The problem was the Wazhazhe lifestyle was different from the Europeans, and for that matter their way of life was different from the other Great Plains people or those of the woodland tribes. Their lifestyle and level of affluence allowed the Wazhazhe nation to make alliances and trade with the Europeans. Instead of challenging the Wazhazhe warriors, the Europeans preferred to make peace and, exchange information.

"Another explanation of great consequence was that they had watched the migration of settlers from the east crossing into their lands. The way the settlers misused the land and destroyed the hunting grounds was repulsive to them, and they believed the land was no longer sacred. The federal government could not or would not stop the migration of settlers from the east.

"At first some of most disobedient members of the Wazhazhe nation tried to drive them out themselves. But it was of no use. Finally most of the land was lost, not through war but in treaties with the English of the east. They were paid some money for the land while the English compensated some of the settlers for their losses of property purportedly destroyed during disagreements with the Wazhazhe warriors."

Joseph had read about the treaties in his school books, except he always thought the books never told the Wazhazhe side of what really happened. He asked his great-grandmother to tell them what she remembered when she was young and asked was it like the books at the English school.

Warmwind said she did not know what the books said; she could only tell what happened during her life.

"For me and those of my generation it was a time of great uncertainty and suffering, but it was also a time of excitement and revolution. There were those among our clan that accepted and welcomed a new lifestyle while others fought to keep the old ways.

"It is the reason my clan was chosen to make the pilgrimage into the valley of the vapors. I am very tired; you will have to excuse me now."

Joseph and Ida Belle left Warmwind's room thinking their great-grandmother had once more left them with more questions about their ancestors. What was the valley of the vapors, and what was the reason for their pilgrimage?

For Joseph, learning about his ancestors would wait until another time. He had been watching the southern sky through his great-grandmother's window; a large thunderstorm was headed toward their ranch.

Joseph found his father and older brothers watching the sky as he came down the stairs. He listened to one of his older brothers say he believed it would be a twister storm. Joseph had heard of the twister storm before. Legends spoke of evil spirits having fun as they raced through the sky whipping the storm into a fierce whirlwind. But that was just a legend, he was sure.

It was decided that turns would be taken that night, watching the storm in case it was a twister. Plans were put in place to release the animals and take shelter in case it was a twister. Ida Belle, her mother, and Great-grandmother were to go to the cave just in case it was a twister.

After some discussion Joseph was to take the first watch; he was to wake one of his older brothers at ten o'clock. Joseph expected it was because of his age and that the storm was some ways off that he was first. Anyway, he was glad to be included and would watch from the front porch.

Joseph had just sat down when Jack was standing before him with the most intense gaze that he had ever seen. It was a gaze that Joseph could not ignore. Jack reeled around, taking a few steps, and then turned to back to see Joseph's response.

When Joseph did not respond he made three sharp barks that Joseph recognized as the same when he was looking at the possum. Joseph, after informing his father, followed Jack past the stables onto the lane leading to the goat and cattle corrals. Jack hurried along the lane, making sure the boy was able to keep up.

In the open plains of the grassland he had often watched such a storm as this one turn into what the cowboys called a tornado. There was an absence of scent in the atmosphere, quietness without the movement of air; yes, there would be a tornado. By the movement of the skies he knew the storm would not disturb the house and stables; it was the corrals of the cattle and goats in the way of the tornado.

Upon reaching the corrals Joseph found the two Great Pyrenees trying to free the goats. He lost no time releasing the goats and cattle within the corrals. Jack immediately drove the cattle down into a narrow but deep valley some distance away. The Great Pyrenees and goats followed noisily along. There within the trees and boulders they were safe.

Jack, unable to find Joseph, returned to the corrals and found him watching a spout forming in the storm a short distance away. Jack raced to Joseph, almost knocking him down in the wind.

Suddenly it became very quiet; both the border collie and the boy ran to take cover within an old, shallow water well. In the distance the lightning lit up the sky, revealing the twister as it was coming closer to the corrals. With each lightning strike the thunder that followed shook the wall of the old abandon well.

Joseph could feel his close companion tremble with each blast from the thunder. What is this, *he thought,* the sentry and protector of the ranch is humbled by thunder? Maybe there is some truth to legends that say it is the spirits racing through the sky that causes the thunder.

Joseph with his back to the wall of the old well slid down, wrapping his arms around his cattle dog. Jack placed his head under Joseph's arm, concealing his eyes and ears.

As Joseph held his companion close to him, the sounds of the storm and the sensation he was feeling began to form words and then phrases in his thoughts. Soon he was reciting them to his friend and companion.

<blockquote>
Do not suffer the weakness of fright;
spirits make fun of our fear in the night.
Let them send the thunder likened to buffalos
racing through the heavens.
</blockquote>

Let them send the winds likened to dark spirits
twisting and howling.
Do not suffer the weakness of fright;
spirits make fun of our fear in the night.
Is it not the ancients that look on to see bravery
at the time our trial?
Is it not the ancients that record for all our courage
at the time of our peril?

For what seemed like forever Joseph stared at the opening in the well above him. He knew the buildings and corrals were being demolished as the wreckage passed over him. Just when he thought the twister had finished its havoc, the opening above was covered by the devastation above.

From within the dark well the wind and rain could be heard above. As Jack regained his composure he tried to resume his standing with what he no longer measured as a boy. Joseph in some way was sorry the storm was over; he had felt the nature of humans and animals become one like never before.

Joseph tried to dislodge the obstructions that were covering the opening to the well. It was of no use, and he sat back down, only to find the well filling with water. In his mind he considered the time they had came into the well, how long the storm had lasted, and how long it would be before it became light outside

It would be at least four hours. His father would search the stables and the cave below. They would find them too late because the water would fill the well before they reached the corrals.

Joseph was right. His father and brothers had searched the stables, the cave, and the surrounding area, believing he would be there. It would have been useless for them to search elsewhere in the dark. They would have to wait until first light to continue their search.

Ida Belle had helped her great-grandmother back to her room, unable to control a feeling of despair. Just as she left her great-grandmother, images of her brother in a dark, wet hole begin to emerge in her thoughts. She raced to her father, asking about her brother. After hearing he was missing, she told her mother of her visions.

Together Ida Belle and her mother went to Warmwind and related to her the events of the night and Ida Belle's visions. Warmwind asked Ida Belle if she still wore the amethyst stone. After hearing that she did, Warmwind said,"Then you do not need me."

Ida Belle removed the stone from beneath her shirt; holding it tightly, she closed her eyes and began to focus on her brother.

Ida Belle could feel the amethyst pulsing from cool to warm, then she whispered to her mother, "I have found him. He is in the old well near the cattle corrals. We must hurry because he is in danger; the water around him is rising very fast."

"Wait!" Her mother cautioned, "What will you tell your father? You had better let me inform him. You can go with your father to make sure they find him."

Ida Belle's mother had quietly watched her daughter grow in the ways of the ancestors and knew this was not the time to let the family know of her gift. As a young girl she too had experienced the gifts of the ancients awaken in her. She was Ida Belle's age when her mother had died from the white man's sickness. In her grief she had given up the ways of the ancestors.

Within a few minutes Ida Belle, her father, and brothers had left the house on their way to the corrals. Why had they not thought of looking for him at the corrals before? The rain and wind was still strong, causing the trip to be difficult.

It was only after reaching the corrals that they realized how much damage the storm had caused. Ida Belle raced to the well, saying she had heard someone calling.

The rain had filled the well to where both Joseph and Jack had to swim in order to stay above the water. Joseph, trying to keep up his courage remembered the chant that filled his mind before. It was as though Jack understood his words and became more at ease until he began to bark very loudly. From beneath the strewn wreckage he had caught the scent of the girl as she came to the well.

After being rescued, Joseph, keeping his composure, acknowledged his sister and thought, How did she know? *It did not matter. She had saved him and his dog. Then he remembered Sadie and asked his father if she was okay.*

It took most of the day to fashion makeshift corrals and to round up the cows and goats. There were only three goats missing. Joseph listened to his father tell him that he would have to wait until tomorrow to search for the goats. He would have to get some rest.

Joseph, unable to rest, returned to the tack room to finished the top figure of his totem. In a state of bewilderment, as he carved the scene of a bear towering over a rushing stream began to emerge.

When he had finished making the final adjustments he realized that Jack and Sadie were both at the window. What he did not realize was that Ida Belle had been watching too but had slipped away before he noticed. Yes, it was her totem too.

CHAPTER FIFTEEN:

SUCCESSFUL STRATEGY OR AN APOLOGY

Hanna cleared her throat as if to say, *We have to talk.* She had begun to feel very comfortable with Sarah. "It is not another mystery; it is just imagery, the spoken language. Please stop trying to listen to your voice when you read."

"I will," Sarah responded, "that is if you explain what you mean about imagery, the spoken language. I don't believe you are talking of mental images created from one's memory or their imagination?

"Is it more like mental images formed in my thoughts as I read the words and that in some way became part of my voice? You are right—the mental images went away when I tried to listen to my voice when reading."

Hanna smiled and said, "It is as you have said; if you would like we can talk about the images that come to me while you are reading. Do you remember the part of the journal when Ida Belle was listening to Joseph tell her about the cougar and the valley?"

"I do," Sarah answered, "although at that time I did not understand and thought whoever wrote the journal was just using their imagination as I was when I read the journal. Sometimes I think I must be imagining everything even now."

Still, she could not reject her thoughts that the journal was in some way interactive with her. Was it not answering the questions and concerns she was experiencing? Okay! She could be mistaken.

Sarah's thoughts turned to the room in the old ranch house; maybe she had not decided to put Ida Belle's things in the small room on her own. Joseph in the journal had described the room in exactly the same way she had arranged it.

She then thought this was silly—did not Warmwind tell Joseph and Ida Belle something about a time when the past and the present would be one? That was what put the thought in her mind. It was intriguing though, the thought that she could be the one to follow Ida Belle "gifted in some way." Was she on her way to become Wazhazhe?

At the dinner table that night most of the discussion was about finding more of clan's sacred objects that was used in ceremonies. Sarah asked if anyone had looked in the cave just below the stables.

Her cousins asked her what cave, and her grandfather looked at her with surprise. Again Sarah found herself the center of attention with complete silence in the room.

John, her grandfather's cousin James nodded his head saying "You know I had forgotten about that cave.

"It's all grown over with brush now. We have all been past it many times and did not know it. You are very perceptive to have noticed it."

Sarah said, "Thank you," but thought, *I will have to be more careful from now on.* Another thought passed through her mind: maybe her grandfather and his cousin did not know what was happening to her.

Late that night Sarah devised a plan to find out if the mystery surrounding the family was real or if it was just her imagination. If it was just her imagination then that was okay; she had become good friends with Hanna and enjoyed reading about Joseph and Ida Belle.

However, if it was not her imagination there was so much more she must find out about. The mysterious gift—whoever wrote the journal made it seem like it was almost a customary occurrence or was at least not uncommon. If that were true there would be others in the family besides Hanna that would be gifted, at least one.

The old ranch house was completely torn down, and work had started on the stables. First she would volunteer to help when they removed all the old horse stalls around the old council room. There was sure to be someone who would slip up and give up their identity. If not, she still had the gemstone and the dress.

The next day Sarah wrapped the dress up and found a way, with Hanna's help, to go into the nearest town. She found a shop that would duplicate the dress, using the same beads and similar materials. *This is going to be fun*, she thought. *The ancients can smile on me too.* That night at the evening meal Sarah scrutinized each one to determine who would be her first prey.

At breakfast the following morning she had found her target and volunteered to help him haul off the discarded bits and pieces. This cousin named Will was a few years older than she was, but he had been watching her all through dinner. How hard would it be to get him to tell her everything? After all, was she not a descendant of Warmwind too?

As the day went on Sarah became so involved in the project she almost forgot all about her cause. Her cousin was polite and wanted to know all about her grandfather. Before the evening meal she had agreed to look at his sketches of the ranch and mountains.

She had become the emissary of her timid cousin Will, who was so shy he could not talk to her grandfather. He knew nothing of the mysterious gift.

All was not lost; this evening she would find another member of the family who might possess such a mysterious gift. There was talk around the table of how the renovation was going and what the plans were for the next day.

Sarah was about to give up when she noticed one cousin about her age absorbed in her own thoughts. What was she thinking? Maybe this one who was always trying to be alone was the one. What was her name? Julie.

The next morning at breakfast Sarah volunteered to help Julie prepare and serve the noon meal. She soon found out the work was hard, and there was not much time to talk. The two cousins worked hard and turned the job into an enjoyable occasion. It was a contest to see who could carry as many plates or serve the ice tea without incident. At the end of the day they were great friends.

That evening Sarah began to sense that Hanna did not approve of what she was doing. The perception was true; without any words being said, Sarah began to realize her error. Sarah was miserable when her new friend said she wanted to reveal a secret to her. She almost did not go to the location where they had arranged to meet.

Once there Sarah began to make an apology, but Julie interrupted her saying there was not much time. A boy she liked had sent her a letter, and she wanted Sarah's help in writing him back. She thought Sarah would understand and was her only hope in keeping it quiet, since the others cousins would tease her and make fun.

This time Sarah was not disappointed her cousin was not the one she was looking for, and together they answered the boy's letter. The next day she saddled Misty, and together with Hanna they delivered the letter as promised.

That night at the evening meal Sarah noticed a boy about her age sitting near the door. She had seen him before, or had she? Yes, she remembered he had not become frightened the first night at the old ranch house. He would not be afraid to tell her if the mystery surrounding the family was real.

No! She thought, *Hanna is right* after the near catastrophe she had with her cousin Julie, she would abandon her first strategy and begin planning a new one. She was sure her new friend Julie and her timid cousin Will had no idea of what she was searching for. It would have to be another, more cunning and secretive plan.

She would have to bring that one out by something unexpected and startling. Her idea began to develop when someone had suggested a dance to celebrate when the council room was finished.

Plans were made to use the old wood from the horse stalls for a fire and everyone was to prepare their native ceremonial dress for the dance.

It was just the right occasion for Sarah to wear the new dress and gemstone. She would soon know if there was someone and if it was not her imagination.

The day finally came when the last, finishing touch was completed on the renovation, and the celebration began. Sarah helped prepare the food and served the family and guests. After it became dark she slipped away to change into her ceremonial dress.

Her plan was working perfectly, she thought, until she stepped into the light of the bonfire.

It was like the world had come to an end. The music stopped, some shrieked, others fainted, and others frantically ran away. Sarah ran to her grandfather asking what had happened.

"I believe it is you that has happened," he replied. "Where did you get the dress?"

Sarah explained there was a dress like this one in the room with the basket and journals. The dress shop was able to make a new one using the old dress as a pattern. Slowly some of the others began to come back, amazed how much Sarah looked like Ida Belle. It was not until Hanna brought her a picture of Ida Bella in the same dress with the gemstone around her neck that Sarah understood what had happened.

Sarah apologized to all and ran to the stables to be with Misty, where she could think about what had taken place. *Grandfather's cousin said ever since I came everything has changed. Maybe I should leave.* Misty let out an almost silent neigh and nuzzled the gemstone around Sarah's neck. The dark blue stone began to glow and change color.

Okay, Sarah thought, *maybe I do look like Ida Belle, and maybe Joseph, Jack, and Sadie are as it is written in the journal.* The stone was real enough, although she had seen stones change color before; it had something to do with one's energy being transferred to the stone.

She would go to her grandfather and explain everything. Maybe now he could tell her more about why they came to the ranch. Sarah's grandfather was waiting for her on the front porch of the ranch house.

There was nothing more he could tell his granddaughter, only reassure her that it was not her imagination; what she was experiencing was real and very real. Had he not seen her once before in his dream wearing a dress like the one she was wearing tonight?

The next morning Sarah waited until only a few remained before entering the kitchen for breakfast. It was as though nothing had happened except she could feel her presence took on a different atmosphere.

She was no longer a young girl of sixteen years. She was there with them and not there with them at the same time—except for Hanna, who with an almost apologetic smile said, "It is as it should be."

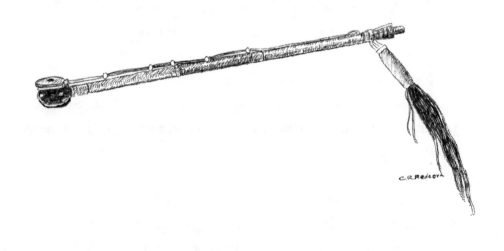

Part Four:

JOURNEY TO THE LAND OF THE VAPORS

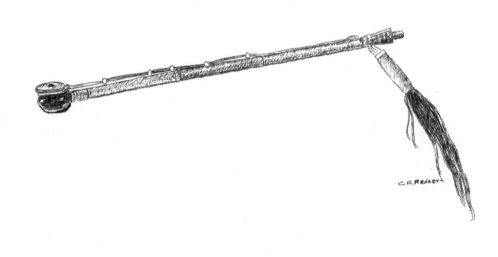

Chapter Sixteen:

Weeping springs

That afternoon Warmwind waited patiently for the boy to become comfortable alongside his sister before speaking first in her native tongue and then in the language the boy could comprehend easier.

"You must forgive me if I speak to you of sad experiences in the days of my youth. Please remember, sometimes the past and present, they are one—that is why I will speak of a time of my youth.

"It was the summer of my twelfth year, when the tribal leaders ceremoniously visited my family's dwellings. They spoke of the unrest throughout the Wazhazhe nation. From the east, unwelcome Indian nations crossed the Missouri River to ravish our hunting grounds. The three great foreign powers no longer honored their agreements and quarreled."

Because of this, the leader had chosen her grandfather's people, the Bear Clan, to make a journey into the valley of Nowasalon "the breath of healing."

"It was a great honor for my family. Nowasalon is a sacred valley hidden by mist from warm, healing springs. The journey would take several days over the mountains, across rivers, and through dense forest.

"On our third night, we reached a steam fed by water dripping from the suspended cliffs within a deep gorge. At the campfire that night, I remember the storyteller recounted a legend of the weeping springs."

Warmwind gave an inward sigh and asked for their permission for her to tell the story as she remembered it. The twins eagerly gave this.

"It was long after the sun went down when all had eaten and the animals were safely secured for the night. As was the custom, the braves built a campfire for the night. This night as we all bedded down in our blankets around the campfire, the reflection of the fire merged with the water dripping down from the face of the cliffs.

"Ghost-like figures appeared to beckon to us from the walls of the cliffs. The water no longer sang a song of wonder but of human weeping. To calm our fears, the storyteller rose from his blanket and began to speak.

"'A long time ago this land was once a beautiful prairie. A wondrous river gave life to streams that flowed all year long. The Great Spirit so blessed the land that the earth yielded an abundant harvest.

"'The Indian tribes living in the area found the streams flourishing with fish, the woods harbored ever kind of game animal, and wild fruit and berries grew everywhere. All this the Great Spirit gave without asking anything in return with one exception" it is forbidden to enter a sacred cave from which the river flowed.'"

Joseph had to speak up. "If the Great Spirit did not want the Indian tribe to go into the cave, why did he place it there? The cave could have been hidden high on a mountain or something."

Ida Belle was saying, "Joseph, please! Be quiet!" when Warmwind said it was a good question.

"To test their devotion, the Great Spirit withheld the one thing from the Indian tribe that would certainly arouse their curiosity." After given Joseph a knowing look, Ida Belle asked Warmwind if she would take up the story again. Warmwind had become weary and said she could continue the story tomorrow; for now she must rest.

Both Ida Belle and Joseph were awake and in the kitchen before the morning meal was prepared. For the first time in his life, Joseph became conscious of his sister's thoughts but wondered if it was his ability or that of his sister. When their mother asked what was happening, both were silent and could not answer.

Ida Belle fixed a plate of food for Warmwind and slowly went up the stairs. Something was bothering her. This morning Warmwind was already out of bed and sitting in the chair. Before Ida Belle had a chance to ask, she said, "It is not Joseph that you should worry about.

"He will encounter shadowy glimpses of the other worlds but is too strong to fall into the trickster's traps. It is good Joseph has a companion who also knows the trickster and all his tricks; unfortunately the malicious one lingers among us.

"It is right that you suspect the trickster had a devious role in the legend of the dripping springs. In some way, the mischievous one becomes a reflection of our worst needs and fears. It is the most wicked and depraved spirits that you must worry about; they roam around the world searching for gifted ones to corrupt."

Warmwind became silent and watched Joseph as he was leaving for the stables. Sarah followed her gaze and realized the image of Joseph and his dog conveyed far more to Warmwind than she could have imagined.

As Joseph came into the stables, he realized the three missing goats must be the same ones that had caused trouble before. No doubt they had wandered off and became lost. There would not be any tracks after the wind and rain. It was strange how the Great Pyrenees had not taken charge of them.

Sadie and Jack were waiting for Joseph as he reached the stables. They both had sensed a new adventure and were anxious to begin. All that day the trio searched the ridges and valleys above the ranch house and stables; there was not a trace of the three goats. Joseph was not to give up; he would search across the river the next day.

After finishing his evening meal, Joseph found Ida Belle with Warmwind in her room. He had not noticed their conservation suddenly ended as he entered the room. Ida Belle was now engaged in an activity that required complete secrecy. Warmwind had warned her, "Even though you will use the knowledge I am passing on to you for good; Joseph will not accept it."

Warmwind sat in her chair and asked, "What were we talking about last night?"

Joseph immediately replied, "You were telling us about the legend of the weeping springs. The Great Spirit had forbidden the native Indian tribe from entering a sacred cave to test their loyalty."

She had not forgotten; she could proceed with her story knowing Joseph was interested.

"I remember the spiritual leader telling us not to be afraid. We would not be harmed. It was then we were able to listen to the legend without thinking about the ghost-like figures moving about the face of the waterfall. As the fire grew weaker, we could no longer see the figures or hear the weeping of the dripping water.

"As I remember the storyteller told us for many years the young had asked questions about the forbidden cave and wondered about its mystery. Unable to control their curiosity, they asked the storytellers what was inside the cave.

"The storytellers declared that it was the entrance to an enchanted world of elves where beautiful lodges lined the banks of a river of gold. Here all the needs of the people were provided for; there was not strife or worry, and men and women occupied themselves with what pleased them.

"As time went on the tribe became obsessed with the need to explore the cave. They ignored the wise men's warnings that reminded them of the Great Spirit's demand. The foolish young braves built many canoes that carried the entire tribe on a journey up the river. Soon the river current became swifter and more dangerous.

"At last, they paddled their way into the recesses of the dark passage. When the last canoe had entered the great cave, there was a heavy rumble of thunder, and a great earthquake sealed the cave forever.

"The Great Spirit then caused the earth to push upward, causing the prairie to become a mountain range. The peaceful river changed its course and wound its way through the mountains.

The frightened and unhappy Indians found themselves in a prison that was to remain forever closed. They felt great sorrow for their disobedience, and their eyes became fountains of tears. Eventually the tears filled the caverns and seeped through the cracks of the mountains, where we see them dripping sadly to this day.

"It was agreed by all after the storyteller finished the legend of weeping springs that there would not be any more wood placed on the fire that night. Before leaving the campsite the next morning, many of the young braves search the cliffs and stream for signs to prove their bravery.

"*As we traveled out of the gorge, no one turned to look back except myself and the one in our clan called Whitedeer. As we walked together, she asked me if I enjoyed the legend of weeping springs. She had noticed I was not afraid.*"

Joseph told Warmwind, that it was a good legend, it could have happen right in their mountains, as he left the room. Asking himself, How could such a prairie exist? *his first thought was that it would be okay to have everything you wanted just handed to you.*

Then he changed his mind; he enjoyed the challenge of hunting for game that was as smart and as strong as he was. He would have pleaded with Wakonda to make the animals and birds as free as he was.

Ida Belle stayed behind, and when Joseph was well away she asked, "Great-grandmother, that was not all that happened that night, was it? Was this the same Whitedeer lost with the clan's sacred bundles?"

Warmwind answered, "Yes, she is the same.

"When the ghost figures appeared on the cliffs Whitedeer had moved her blanket close to mine. In our village Whitedeer lived a quiet, solitary life; my father had invited her counsel many times. I was honored to be in her presence."

Warmwind, aware her great-granddaughter would not be content with her account of what had happened, continued, "The gift of nature's wisdom and the spirit is not given, only awakened." It was all Warmwind would say.

It was exactly what Ida Belle wanted to hear. She did not know what had awakened such a consciousness in her. It must also lie deep within her brother's subconscious too.

Chapter Seventeen:

Chewaukla: "Sleepy Waters"

The next day Joseph and his companions searched across the river among the cattle for any signs of the three missing goats; still, they found nothing. Jack and Sadie were beginning to lose interest, the idea of spending that much time looking for goats was not sensible. Joseph would not give up; he would keep looking, but for now he wanted to find out more about Nowasalon.

Warmwind had noticed a feeling of superiority in Ida Belle's movements as she left her room the night before. She remembered her first insight into the existence of mystical beings. She had come so close to losing the gifts of the ancients.

She shut her eyes and remembered a previous time long ago, as she and her clan visited the Valley of the Mystical Vapors. She would reveal that to Ida Belle later on. For now, she would have to let her make her own way.

Warmwind's thoughts turned to the trickster, the resourceful one. How often had she observed the trickster defy time and space, change form, and then disappear into the world of spirits? She remembered their paths crossing many times.

Understanding and recognizing the elusive one would be Ida Belle's most enjoyable challenges. She was confident Ida Belle would triumph over the imaginative, troublesome, and comical trickster.

That evening Joseph asked, "What happened after the clan left Weeping Springs, and why was the clan sent to Nowasalon?"

Warmwind replied, "I would first tell you of our first night in the Valley of the Vapors.

"It was the first day we camped alongside others not of our people. The youngest members of our clan were puzzled why we would camp at such an unmanageable canyon full of large boulders and with water everywhere.

"As we set up camp, the wiseman told us all tribes shared the valley of the vapors. It was a sacred place of peace given to all tribes by the Great Spirit."

Joseph asked, "Was this place called Nowasalon?"

"No," Warmwind answered. "The place was called Chewaukla, which means 'Sleepy Water.'

"We had only to travel through the canyon to reach Nowasalon. That night and the next day, we were to remain camped by a small stream fed by a number of cold springs. That evening, all along the stream campfires lit up the canyon. I had never seen such a gathering before. There was one very large campfire visited by people of many tribes and some foreigners too.

"All night long, the storytellers told an account of their tribe's ventures and of their accomplishments while the elders drank water from the sacred spring.

"During the next day, the older ones gossiped and talked of the weather and current events. I could easily move around from one campsite to another, hearing accounts in the lives of different tribes. I made many new friends, several from tribes who we sometimes fought with over hunting grounds.

"When night came, my grandfather, the clan leader, commanded that I was to attend to his fireplace. I was able to leave only when accompanied *by Whitedeer. I did not mind; it was a special place of beauty apart from at night when all the eerie sounds began.*

"The storytellers said it all started long ago when a young brave and maiden from two different nations became too friendly." Warmwind gave out a big yawn, saying, she was tired and would have to sleep now.

Joseph and Ida Belle helped Warmwind to her bed and quietly left the room. As they walked to the stairs, Joseph said, "Now we will have to wait until tomorrow to find out about the eerie sounds and what happened to the two from the different nations. Do you think she is doing that on purpose?"

Ida Belle answered, "Oh no, you could tell how fast she went to sleep."

A complete feeling of well-being came over Warmwind as she had listened to her two young great-grandchildren's conversation. She could sleep at ease knowing the boy was very smart and the girl had exceeded her greatest expectations.

Jack was up early the next morning. He had lain awake most of the night listening to the two Great Pyrenees warning all predators to keep their distance. The two giant dogs still confused him. They could do anything they wanted. Yet, they stayed with the goat herd; together they guarded them all night, and then they took turns guarding them during the day while the other slept. He was sure the two of them could easily destroy anything in the forest.

For some time he had watched men fencing in a large field along one side of a new corral. Each morning he had looked over their work and considered what the purpose of the structure was. It was nothing like what he had seen before.

Today he recognized it to be an area for the goats, made to keep other animals out and to keep the goats in. In his exploration of the enclosure, he had found a number of weak places. He would keep them in mind.

As Jack returned to the barn, thoughts of the boy, his sister, the two horses, and the two Great Pyrenees pleased him. It would have been a much easier time working cattle back on the grasslands of the prairie. He liked the cowboys and herding cattle; all the same, there was a need for him here in this wilderness, especially with the mystical one around. What he had not figured out was the cat that he had seen at the stables one night was not an ordinary cat.

As the day proceeded, to Jack's amazement the afternoon moved forward in a very pleasing way. The goat herd behaved reasonably while the boy and girl went about looking for herbs and other plants. The two horses had become companions, sharing their allegiances between their riders and each other. The two Great Pyrenees while protecting the goats had taken alternating time off to hunt for small game.

Yes, Jack believed he was at home with his adopted family, and he accepted the importance of being their guardian—although there was still the mystical cat that most often he could not catch a glimpse of; as a consequence he was sure it could not be an ordinary farm animal. He was sure it was not the mystical trickster either.

It was a serious occasion at the evening meal for Ida Belle. That day the family had learned their oldest brother, Alvin, would have to report to the army for his physical.

Still, the family's main concern was the cutting horse competition and how would they carry on. They would deal with other situations later if necessary.

Both Ida Belle and Joseph finished their meal quickly, hurrying to Great-grandmother's room to ask her about their brother. Once there, Ida Belle's fears gave way to Warmwind's reassurances that it was as it should be. It was time for their brother to find his personal self-awareness and take on personal responsibility for inner self, nature, and spirit.

Joseph was not sure of what all that meant, but if she was saying he should become a warrior fighting for his family, he agreed.

Ida Belle had heard something much different. Her oldest brother was not to go into the army and would not remain on the ranch. Only by reacquainting himself to the natural world of nature and spirituality would he know his most personal, divine self. Then awareness, guidance, and decisive power would be his to live his life without weakness, fear, or temptation.

Joseph was anxious for Warmwind to return to the time she had spent at Chewaukla. It sounded like a place he would like to visit someday; even the eerie sounds sounded interesting to him.

He thought somehow the young brave and maiden Warmwind had talked of, must have drunk some of the sleepy water by mistake and wandered off. It probably would be a legend like the about the weeping springs. Ida Belle would like that.

Joseph asked, "Great-grandmother, at Chewaukla how did the warriors from the other tribes dress, and had they brought their war ponies with them?"

Warmwind replied, "No, the warriors that came with them were there to hunt game and protect their clans. They put away their weapons of war and competed in ball games or wrestling matches. Sometimes they would join the dancing."

After answering Joseph's questions, Warmwind returned to the time of her journey to Nowasalon. She asked the twins what was she saying when they ended last night. Ida Belle reminded her that the storyteller had just told the clan the eerie sounds began after a young brave and maiden had become too friendly. "Was that because they drank the sleepy water?"

"No," Warmwind replied. "Only those in poor health and the elderly drank of the sleepy waters. On such a joyful event, the young and healthy *did not want to drink the sleep-inducing water. As with other tribes, we came to Chewaukla for its great medicine and healing powers."*

Ida Belle had to ask, "What did the young brave and maiden have to do with the eerie screams?"

Joseph thought, Here it comes: another legend.

Warmwind replied, "Late that night the mournful sounds begin to emerge from the darken forest.

"A medicine man from another tribe began to chant around the campfire; with one sweep of his staff over the fire, a large ball of orange flames leaped into the sky. When the orange flames turned yellow, the medicine man loudly proclaimed the mournful sounds conquered.

"The teller of tales then began to tell the story of Silver Star and Gray Wolf. As you know there is a truce among all the peoples who come to drink the healing waters. There were times when the peace was not always honored, because of some difference of belief or jealousy.

"What was most unacceptable and not tolerated occurred: Gray Wolf of a tribe from the east became attracted to Silver Star of a tribe from the north. Silver Star returned his affection and wanted only to be with him.

"Their fathers objected to their passion and commanded they marry someone from their own tribe. They could not accept their fathers' wishes and stole away each night to be together. One night, when Silver Star went to meet Gray Wolf, he did not come. All night she waited for Gray Wolf; still he did not come.

"The next morning she met hunters who told her Gray Wolf was killed by a panther that lived in the mountains. All day Silver Star roamed the mountains and valleys around Chewaukla, weeping for Gray Wolf. That night she plunged a knife into her heart and died. Some believe the eerie sounds are of Silver Star as she wanders through the ravines searching for Gray Wolf.

"Others say the spirit of Silver Star had turned into a panther to avenge the death of Gray Wolf. It is the eerie sounds of the ghost panther they heard as she hunts for Gray Wolf's killer."

Warmwind said, "The teller of tales had finished his story, and although the eerie sounds continued we were not afraid. Silver Star was looking for the panther that killed Gray Wolf, not us.

"It is time for me to sleep now—we will talk of the clan's arrival at Nowasalon tomorrow."

Ida Belle and Joseph helped Warmwind to her bed and left her rooms not saying anything, with the words "Silver Star" occupying their thoughts.

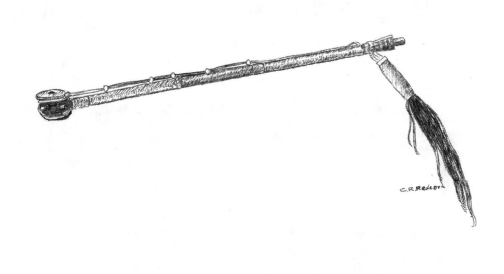

Chapter Eighteen:

Amethyst stone

Ida Belle was in the kitchen early the next morning. This morning, as she helped her mother prepare the morning meal, questions she would ask Warmwind were methodically planned and rehearsed. In the past her mystical insights and premonitions had always been just an amusement. It had been entertaining to know what her brother would do next before he even thought of it. The warmth she had felt with nature, the earth, and all living things was now being challenged.

In the last few days, her life has taken on a more serious nature. She was now experiencing the ways of ancient gifted ones and felt the enormous weight of that responsibility. She did not know what was expected from her or who would expect it of her. She would not give up the friendship of her brother or the love and the spontaneous, natural world of her family.

Ida Belle had prepared a plate of food for Warmwind and was leaving the kitchen when her mother said, "Remember, Warmwind was your father's grandmother before she became your great-grandmother."

A smile, only revealed through her eyes, came to Warmwind's wrinkled face as Ida Belle's footsteps could be heard on the stairs. She had become very *weary in her purpose, nevertheless excited that her great-granddaughter was emerging so well.*

Joseph had watched his sister going up the stairs and realized that this day she would not be going out. On his way to the stables, he had decided he would let Silver Star go along with him if she wanted to. It was a happy caravan as the two Great Pyrenees led the way into the most remote valley. The goat herd followed as Jack kept them in line while Joseph, Sadie, and Silver Star followed along behind.

All that day Jack watched as the horses and goats grazed in the pasture, the Great Pyrenees taking turns either sleeping or hunting. Yet, he could feel there was something watching and waiting in the dark undergrowth of the forest. After exploring the area, he lay down beside the boy, who had found an ideal mound of grass to watch the goat herd from.

Joseph's thoughts were not only of the goat herd. He had dismissed the story of Chewaukla as only a legend. It was easily explained as the wind swirling through the cliffs that made the eerie noise. He was worried about his sister. It was strange she would name the horse Silver Star, the same name as the maiden in the story of sleepy waters. Joseph could see Sadie standing alone nearby. Silver Star was not with her.

Ida Belle had noticed her brother as she left the kitchen that morning. To reveal her concerns to him would only have distanced him; if possible she would confide in him sometime later. For now, she must learn as much as she could from Warmwind. A little afraid but full of determination, Ida Belle went to Warmwind.

Warmwind quietly ate her morning meal as Ida Belle laid out her thoughts and questions; now she must clear her mind and choose her word carefully. She remembered long ago when she was experiencing the same emotions as her great-granddaughter. She must only tell her what she asked for. She could never share her experiences, only tell of them.

Warmwind finished her morning meal and said, "You want to know what is expected of you and who would be expecting it of you. I can only tell you what I know. The teller of legends tell us our tribe was divided into two groups, the earth people and the sky people; these two groups emerged to form the children of the middle waters, 'Niukonska.' It is believed the Great Spirit "'Wakonda gave the children of the middle water the gift of all nature's energies and secrets.

"Through the ages, the gift from Wakonda was neglected by some and misused by others. To only a few who remained reverent to Wakonda were the gift passed on to their descendents.

You are a descendent of Niukonska, the children of the middle waters. You are expected to honor Wakonda and guard nature's secrets. It is expected of you to grow in your connection with nature, other worlds, and Wakonda. Remember the legend of the weeping springs and sleepy waters."

Ida Belle, remembering the amethyst stone, asked, "Are the stone's energies harmful?"

Warmwind replied, "No, the stone is not harmful; the energy you see in the stone comes from you as a gift from the ancients. You must maintain a spiritual balance with the earth, sky, and Wakonda to transfer the energy to the stone or possibly another object as well."

Warmwind thought for a moment and then decided to let her great-granddaughter know about the stone. With a voice stressed by her memory of her youth she continued. "I know of the stone Joseph has given to you. It was not by accident Joseph found the stone.

"Many years ago, I lost the stone while crossing the mountains. It was in the early days of my marriage to your great-grandfather. It was a dreadful time in our history; our leaders signed treaties to relinquish land from what is now known as Missouri, Oklahoma, and Arkansas.

"Later, what was left of us was expected to move west into a reservation . Instead of staying at the reservation, your great-grandfather and I married *and returned to the Ouachita Mountains, making our home where you now are living.*

"Believing the Great Spirit had abandoned us, I neglected the stone, losing my spiritual balance with nature and the Great Spirit. I had returned to the campsite where I lost the stone many times.

"The stone must have remained a dark green color, blending into the forest. I remember the stone had seven sides, each side of the stone requiring a different energy level needed to change appearance."

Ida Belle interrupted her great-grandmother, asking, "What will I be called by others?"

Warmwind thought for a while and then said, "I do not know. When I was young, some of our nation had trouble dealing directly with the energies of nature. It was the custom for them to visit a gifted one for guidance. In the world of today, questions of nature and the other worlds are seldom sought after. It may not be necessary for you to be known to others."

Ida Belle heaved a sigh of relief. She had already made up her mind it would not be anybody's affair but hers and maybe her twin brother's. She would learn the ways of a gifted one and journey to the other world in search of nature's wisdom. If her path crossed that of someone in need of help, she would use her abilities to help them.

She thanked Warmwind and left the room, sensitive to the stress of their conversation on her great-grandmother. She had decided it would be best if she found somewhere to be alone and think. On her way out of the house, she stopped long enough to bring the small basket containing the amethyst stone.

On her way to the stables, she remembered Silver Star should have gone to graze with Sadie. Before she could make other plans, a whinny came from the stables. Ida Belle ran to the stables to find her horse waiting for her. She did not bother to put on the saddle, just snapped two leather reins into the halter ring.

As she rode off, Ida Belle recalled where a rock formation spanned nearly all the way across the river. The water would be spilling over only at one side of the rock structure, just like miniature waterfall. It was a secluded location where she would not be disturbed.

After reaching the stream, Ida Belle unsnapped the reins from the halter to let Silver Star graze in the field nearby. She found a site along the face of the rock formation where she could sit with her legs over the water below and see the waterfall into a pool below.

For a few minutes, Ida Belle let her mind follow a leaf over the waterfall and float down into the pool below where it came in and out of a whirlpool then bobbed up and down as it floated down the river.

Ida Belle examined the basket made from reeds very much like those growing around the stream. She could feel the energy traveling through her hands into the basket. With eagerness and some reservations, Ida Belle opened the cover to see one side of the stone glow a bright pink color.

Unable to resist its allure, she removed the amethyst stone from its basket. The warmth and beauty of the stone replaced the doubt lingering in her mind. The rays of pink light from the stone radiated the sense of clarity and of confirmation. It was as though time had stopped and an unending stream of thoughts and awareness came into her conscious.

"Yes," Ida Belle exclaimed, "the stone is everything Great-grandmother said and more." She was now certain that through her energy the stone had radiated the emotions and concerns she was experiencing. A feeling of a quiet but extremely fulfilling appreciation came over her; had the stone helped save her brother's life, surely it would only bring good to her and others. It was also very humbling as she remembered her feelings of self-importance.

In the past, the gift of the ancients in some way had separated her from her family. She knew they had always loved her, yet she had felt a veiled importance given to her she never understood. It was all very clear to her now. Gently placing the stone back into the basket, she called to Silver Star.

On her ride back to the stable, she carefully considered how she must conduct herself, especially around her twin brother. If she wanted to appear ordinary, she would have to live a shadowy, dual life. She quickly fed Silver Star and returned to the house, determined that she would take on more responsibilities around the house.

That evening the family was surprised as Ida Belle helped her mother prepare and serve the evening meal, although not a word was spoken. Thoughts of Ida Belle's new demeanor diminished as conversations of ranch life and upcoming events began.

Still, Joseph was uneasy with the change that had come over his sister and only reluctantly became involved in the family discussions. Ida Belle's mother, aware of Ida Belle's new revelation, asked her daughter to see if Warmwind needed anything.

Chapter Nineteen:

The land of vapors

J oseph joined his sister as she went into Warmwind's room. Ida Belle
could only give her brother quick glances before asking Warmwind to
continue her story of Nowasalon. Warmwind nodded. "It was early
in the morning when we reached the trail leading out of the mountains into
the valley of the vapors.

The valley that lay before us was as mysterious as the heavens in the
night. At first I could only see a forest with magical vapors rising from
the treetops to meet the ghost-like clouds reaching down. Then we felt the
warmth of the hot springs flowing out of the mountain crevices into the
waiting pools below. It was there we paused, allowing those affected with
the most perilous ailments to bathe.

As we entered the valley Whitedeer was by my side pointing out,
abundant plant life, novaculite, and other minerals. It had been several
years since her last visit to the land of the healing waters. I could not help
but see the discomfort she was experiencing as we walked along the oddly
constructed buildings and smelly campsites of the foreigners."

I felt sadness and then a renewed determination in her manner.
The once tranquil surroundings she had known had been replaced by the

unruliness and uncertainty brought about by the barbaric foreigners. It was not the first time I had seen foreign people, but it was here in this native land with Whitedeer I realized how different they were. Now I understood the purpose for which we came.

As was the practice of most visitors, we erected small huts near the life-healing water springs. In the center of each hut, a fire within a small basin lined and filled with rocks was sprinkled with water causing steam to fill the hut. We would wrap ourselves in blankets and let the vapors of Nowasalon waters free us of all our ailments.

Still others covered themselves with the extraordinary, health-giving mud from the mineral deposits. One older man suffered from pain in his bones. After covering his body with the mud, he was seen playing games with the younger men. The warriors of our clan filled their packs with the mud for use in future battles. It was believed to give them spiritual powers and added strength. Others bathed or drank from the warm spring waters.

That evening my father told me I was to accompany Whitedeer while in the land of vapors; he did not say anything more. Just as it was getting dark Whitedeer was summoned to the council tent where the clan leaders had assembled. I sat next to Whitedeer, trying to understand what was taking place and to control my emotions.

The next day Whitedeer and I visited many camps of other tribes and even that of the foreigners. At first my presence was questioned, and then as the day went on I would only receive a casual glance. It was like a dream—we were there, and then we were not there. I wondered if Whitedeer could somehow have cast a spell upon everyone around her.

We visited a camp that had come from a place not far south called New Orleans. They told the Spanish had given the land called the Louisianan Territory back to the French. It was good news because the Spanish were difficult to do business with. In my excitement I forgot to follow Whitedeer and became noticed by the camp. We had to leave.

Later that afternoon we visited the camp of a tribe from east of the 'Father of Waters, the Mississippi river.' For many years our nation had encountered their hostilities. They would take advantage of disorder if a war broke out between the North and the South. We visited many more camps as those there paid little attention to us. We even ate from their cooking pots.

That night at the clan council Whitedeer and I again sat silently as the leaders discussed affairs of the clan; it was as though all that we learned that day was mystically imparted to the clan leaders. Most of the conversation centered on the Wazhazhe Nation and what would happen now. I began to understand Whitewind had not cast a spell that day.

The following morning, Whitedeer showed me a secret passageway through a rock formation that opened into a small gorge not far from camp. From the walls of the gorge, a stream of water flowed into a rock basin. Whitedeer said I must drink from the pool of water within the rock basin. With my first drink, stones on the bottom of the pool begin to glisten with all the color of a rainbow.

One stone shined the brightest of all, an amethyst stone glowing with such warmth and beauty that I chose it above the rest. Whitedeer said I chose well. The path we follow is in the choices we make. From reeds that grew around the pool, I wove a small basket to hold the amethyst stone and keep it from harm.

The rest of the day Whitedeer instructed me in the art of herbal remedies. For two days, we searched and collected more than fifty different plants, each one to cure a different disease or provide relief from a painful ailment. There was so much I did not know.

On the following day, Whitedeer woke me before sunrise, saying, 'Get up—we will go to a place that is far.' This day two horses were waiting for us along with food for the day. We reached an uninhabited, forbidding area where the earth was without color and barren.

As we traveled on, we reached a place of great destruction at the base of a mountain. Whitedeer would only say it was a gift of the Great Spirit. We made our way through the strange land until we came to where mysterious dust, beautiful gems, and minerals swelled up from deep in the earth.

It was here that Whitedeer began instructing me in the use of different minerals and their benefits. From her pack, she removed small sticks of wood and built a small fire. After identifying a different mineral, she would throw it on the fire to demonstrate its powers.

When we returned to our campsite, my father met us, asking if we had seen my older sister Willow. All in our clan was deeply concerned. There was hearsay that she was sneaking out at night to meet a brave from another nation. This was a grave defiance of tribal laws; a marriage was always approved by the village leader and only for those of the nation three tribes.

That night at the council the elders spoke of what they had learned. All the clan quit their activities and returned to camp. A messenger was chosen and sent back to the village with news of what they had discovered. Finding Willow would have to wait; Grandfather assembled his clan and declared we would be leaving the next day.

Late at night Willow came to my blanket and said she was leaving that night with a Kansa brave she had met. They would be traveling to a beautiful county her husband-to-be had found while hunting along the White River. Just as quickly as she had come, she vanished into the night.

Early that morning before dawn Grandfather woke me saying, The Great Spirit visited him in a dream. He told me, 'In the dream, you were standing with me as the nation of Niukonska passed through many trials. My grandfather had bestowed a great honor on me. I assured him I would be his servant as long as he needed me. The journey back to their village was one of mourning and much deliberation.

Warmwind sighed and said that was all she would say about Nowasalon; the knowledge she had learned at Nowasalon would be of great importance to her clan. She would like to say a prayer to their ancestors and await the day she went to meet them."

Both Ida Belle and Joseph interrupted at the same time, with Ida Belle saying, "There is so much more you must tell us to keep our promise."

Warmwind again asked to be alone and said it was not for her to say when she would leave them.

How could she make the events of a time long past in her youth become clear and understandable to her great-grandchildren? Even now her thoughts of that time were not many and sometimes confusing.

Joseph just shook his head, thinking they probably went back to the village to get more warriors. He would have covered himself with the healing mud that gives spiritual powers and gone after Willow.

Then again, if everyone covered themselves with the healing mud, would not they all have the spiritual powers? As Joseph went off to his room, he was certain his sister and great-grandmother were living in a fantasy world. He did enjoy the stories.

Ida Belle had stayed behind, waiting for Joseph to enter his room. She had many questions for her great-grandmother. The first and the most important, "What happened in the secret gorge when you drank from the pool of water? I know it must be the same amethyst stone my brother found in the mountains. What would have happened if you chose another stone?"

Warmwind answered, "There were many shiny stones in the pool. There were diamonds, opals, and other beautiful stones that reached out to me. Each stone would have given my life in a different meaning. The amethyst stone both vibrated passion and radiated a colorful glow of energy unlike the other stones, beautiful but cold and forbidding.

"*That which is not alive in nature possesses the purest form of nature's certainties and truths. In my choice of the amethyst stone I had begun to follow inner wisdom inherited from the ancients and spirits. It is in the pursuit of nature's energies that we become one with our ancestors.*"

Ida Belle had always thought she was just like her brother, her family, and everyone else, simply gifted in other ways. That is until now; what had amused her before as a child now forecast a future she could not have imagined. Now she knew her way of life would take on proportions beyond her childhood visions. In her solitude she joined the lives of countless ancestors that preceded her.

Sarah closed the journal, thinking Ida Belle had come to the same place on the river and maybe sat right where she was sitting right now. The journal was in many ways corresponding to her life. It was all very strange.

She wondered, was the journal real, was it written for her? Or maybe like the amethyst stone the words were coming from energy within her. How could this be possible?

No, maybe the energy might in some way come from within her, but not the knowledge. Yes, it is almost like a dream where the past and present are one. Only the water bubbling in the stream and the wind blowing through my hair is very much real.

Something within her examined every experience she could remember. It was not that she was more perceptive than other children; she knew that now. She felt for Ida Belle who, knowing of the gift she possessed, had lived a life in some way apart from her family. As far as being gifted in some ways, that was true; was she not gifted too?

"May I speak?" came the soft voice of Hanna. "I must tell you that feeling the presence of is a gift; it is not that we are gifted in any way. No matter what you read or hear, there are not any sacred places or mystic beings either, just the Great Spirit Wakonda is everywhere and in all things."

Sarah quickly replied, "I am glad you are here; I am not convinced that you are really only twelve years old. I am not going to ask how you must have known what I was thinking.

"I will ask" can you explain what is bothering me now?"

"That is true," said Hanna, taking a long, deep breath. "It is the invisible world and all the possibilities of it that distract you."

"Of course, you must have already read the journal," Sarah said, dismissing her suspicions.

Sarah had almost finished the fourth part of the journal. Was it all real? Warmwind, Joseph, Ida Belle, and all the rest in the journal were her ancestors; she knew that. And yes it was possible the gift of nature's wisdoms was awakening in her

"You must be patient to know of such things," Hanna assured her.

I should have known, Sarah thought; it's probably written later on in the journal.

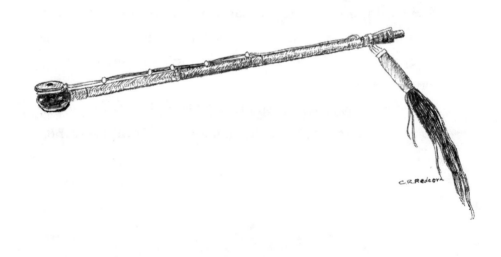

Chapter Twenty:

Osage village sketch

The next day Sarah found her grandfather making a sketch of a native Indian village he had labeled as Osage Village. Sarah at once noticed some parts that she thought were not exactly right. Her grandfather began to revise the sketch, making changes precisely to the same parts she had found amiss and a with a knowing smile said, "Thank you. Between the both of us we will get it right."

Sarah was just about to ask her grandfather if this would be a good time for them to visit the town called Osage. She suspected that was his objective and the sketch was his way of organizing his thoughts for the trip when her grandfather said, "Of course it will be all right if Hanna accompanies us today."

It was clear now to Sarah this was not an ordinary vacation but an adventure her grandfather had carefully planned for them, or had he? How could he know about Hanna, Quinton, and the rest of the cousins? If only she knew what was her role in the adventure.

On her way to find Hanna, Sarah thought, Yes, Hanna is a little strange—wouldn't anyone who lost their mother and father when they were four years old be? In some way she felt they had become more than friends.

The day was warm and sunny as James drove out of the mountains and along the Buffalo River, which at times seemed more like a lake than a river. However, Sarah was not thinking about the scenery; her thoughts were of Hanna.

"Would you like to tell us about your grandmother and where you lived before coming to the ranch?" she asked Hanna. "We would like to know, that is if it is something you would like to talk about."

"If you would like," Hanna answered. "But please know that in my grandmother's house it was expected that one would speak only when asked or if it was necessary. My grandmother followed the ways of her parents and those of their parents.

We rarely went to the towns or villages. At first it was difficult. The food we ate was mostly from the land—you know, like greens and herbs. Grandmother raised some farm animals, cows, chickens, and geese."

Sarah had to ask, "What about television or music?"

"There was music," Hanna answered with a slight pause. "Some of the close relatives played the violin or the harmonica; it was different than what I have heard since coming to the ranch. Their music was about their experience with nature or of their religious feelings."

Sarah felt a close connection with Hanna and was eager to discover more about her and her grandmother. She asked, "What about school and your friends?"

Hanna answered, "Our school was small and much disciplined. I often thought what it would be like having someone my own age to talk to."

You do now, Sarah thought, *although I think I am a little older.*

"I have often wondered about the medications that can be made from plants and minerals," James said, making it sound more like a question than an assertion.

"It is so," Hanna responded. "It was my task to search the woods for the exact plant root or leaf to make a medication. I do miss that. But not the part when the fat of a goose or another animal had to be used in making the medication."

Later neither Sarah nor her grandfather could hold back their disappointment when the little settlement of Osage came into view. This could not have been the site of the historic Indian village they were looking for.

They had not expected a lot, maybe a post office and a few buildings, but it was disturbing how different it was from the vision that James had so meticulously captured in his sketch.

In a short time an acceptable site was found to verify the landscape; the sketch was not that of the surrounding scenery. There could be no doubt; all agreed that the sketch did not in any way look like what they were seeing. Sarah and her grandfather could only stare at the sketch, each unable to comprehend what had gone wrong.

Suddenly Sarah had the realization that Hanna knew of a place that looked like that of the sketch.

It was then Hanna said, "Yes, I have been there, a place like the one in the sketch. 'The village' is now only an image, and I thank you for the gift. What is beyond my understanding is that you have revealed the sacred burial grounds so well. The river is not the Buffalo River; it is the White River, that of the Wazhazhe people."

James believing Hanna's words about the burial grounds had distressed Sarah called out, "Sarah, Sarah, are you all right?" It was not Hanna's words that surprised Sarah; on the contrary it was that she had in some way become conscious of what Hanna was thinking. She remembered the times when Hanna had responded to her thoughts just as she had to Hanna's today.

"I am all right," Sarah answered. "It's just that so much is happening that is difficult to understand. Do not worry about me.

"Let's go on and find the place Hanna has spoken of. Would it be better if Hanna rode in the front seat so she can show us the way?" Sarah's thoughts turned to the journal; there were three more parts to the journal left, and only a few weeks left before she would have to leave for school.

Hanna began by telling James she could probably find the place in the sketch if he could take them to where the White River and Buffalo River joined just above the mountains.

James asked, "Do you remember a town or village near where the rivers meet?"

"Yes," Hanna answered. "It is named North Fork I think."

Sarah was glad she had asked to ride in the back seat where she could think. What if whoever wrote the journal was somehow interacting with her in some subliminal way and in time lost contact? Or maybe it was just the energies from within her bringing everything out. She must finish the journal before going home; at another time and place it might all be lost to her.

She began to think about when she would be going home. What of Hanna? Hanna, she was different: sometimes she seemed older and wiser than herself and at other times the friend and younger sister she always wanted. How could she give up the close bond she felt growing between them?

She would ask her grandfather if there was something that could be done.

Sarah's thoughts were cut short when Hanna whispered, "We are crossing the White River now. Sir, it is not far. You must go through the next town to a small road that follows the river around the mountains. It is along that road I am sure we will find what you have drawn in your sketch."

"Thank you, Hanna," James exclaimed. "I can see the small road on the map."

It seemed like time stood still to Sarah before Hanna, motioning toward the mountains said, "It is there where the river bends into the mountain. The climb is difficult at first but becomes easier a little father on. If you like we can pick some greens and herbs along the way."

James found a place to park the car that would not be observed by anyone driving down the road. "Do not worry," Hanna said with a slight smile. "No one will bother with us while we are here."

Sarah thought, *Okay but it is a long walk back to the nearest town.*

James and Sarah happily noted and picked the special plants that Hanna located and identified for them as they move closer to the river.

Hanna, with the most serious expression Sarah had ever seen before said, "Sir, I must honor you; I had not realized, until now, how your sketch is a sign of how gifted you must be."

James quickly brought out the sketch and along with Sarah moved to where Hanna was standing; neither one could say a word as they compared the sketch to the surrounding panorama. It was all there— the river, the mountains, the landscape, and what neither James nor Sarah had realized: the burial grounds.

"Is that what I think it is?" James asked, pointing to a circle of rocks that was only just visible near the mountain's crown.

"It is," answered Hanna. He had sketched the landscape not exactly knowing why he had drawn the rock in that particular area.

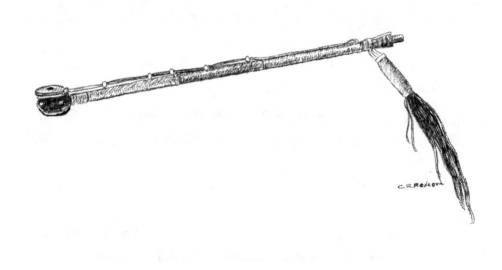

Part Five:

NEW TRADITIONS FOR AN UNWAVERING CULTURE

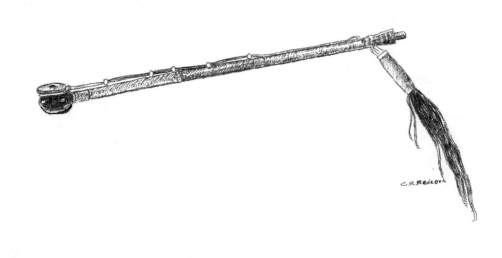

Chapter Twenty-one:

Adjusting to an expanding world

Warmwind awoke the next morning as the sun began to filter into her room. From her window she watched the panoramic view as shades of darkness gave way to the subtle, soft light. A new scene appeared with each moment that passed. The sky lightened into a cheerful blue with featherlike clouds drifting aimlessly about.

She watched as the cattle dog resumed his watch over the ranch at his advantage site above the house and stables. She could feel his self-assured confidence. Suddenly Ida Belle was there opening the window to let the morning air into her room. It is a beautiful morning, *Warmwind thought, but was it nature's gift or that of her great-granddaughter?*

Ida Belle removed the leather pouch from her pocket and placed it gently over her great-grandmother's head, positioning it to lie comfortably within her reach. There was no need for explanations or purpose.

Ida Belle left her great-grandmothers room with a new purpose; with ease she moved about the family, fulfilling her activities with little notice from others while observing every facet of life.

Joseph had left the house early that morning; there was still the mystery of the three missing goats. Maybe a predator slipped past the two Great

Pyrenees dogs. That did not make sense because they were young and quick; a predator would have selected an older or weaker goat. He had to know for sure.

Sadie was anxiously waiting for the boy to come into the stables. She had become eager to be with her two friends. She had enticed the cattle dog the day before to sprint through the fields and woods with her. Both pony and cattle dog missed their human companion. That morning Joseph could hear her calling to him as he left the house. Jack joined the boy and his Indian pony as they left the stables.

It was as if they were one as they traveled along the narrow road leading to the goat corals. Together they experienced an irresistible sensation of freedom. The feeling was soon diminished after they came in sight of the goat herd. The two Great Pyrenees were blocking three young goats from reaching the herd. Jack instantly knew they were the three missing goats that caused all the problems before. Sadie just did not care and could not understand what all the fuss was about.

Joseph could see the big dogs had a problem with the three goats and after a head count rationalized they clearly must have miscounted before. Where else could they have come from? He was amazed they had found their way back to the herd. It was still a mystery why they were prevented from returning to the herd. With some reservations Jack moved the goat herd to a protected area undamaged by the storm.

Jack and Sadie encouraged the boy into finding a new adventure while the goat herd foraged. Joseph remembered a grove of wild cherry trees growing father up the mountain slope whose fruit should have ripened now. The wild cherry trees had been damaged by the storm with some of the branches fallen to the ground. Jack at first found the wild cherries a bit sour but soon learned to eat only the darkest ones. Sadie found that all the cherries and even the leaves tasted agreeable.

Jack, still a little suspicious of the three young goats, caught sight of them leaving the herd. Joseph, seeing his cattle dog in a stalking stance, followed his gaze down to where the mischievous goats were disappearing into the underbrush. He then turned his attention to the Great Pyrenees calmly watching over the goat herd. It must be they are protecting the main herd, *he thought.*

Jack knew better; the big dogs did not believe they were from their herd and were glad to see them go. He was curious to where they were going, and he could tell the boy was too. With a little persuasion Sadie was ready to join her companions and follow the goats. Tracking the goat was easy with the landscape still wet from the storm.

The trail led them through the underbrush onto a rock formation where the tracks disappeared. Both Jack and the boy looked for any sign of their trail, but none could be found. Jack closed his eyes with the full awareness of the boy's intense look. Joseph also was aware his dog knew he was thinking, "Ha, is this the greatest hunting dog ever?"

Jack regained his self-respect when Joseph gave up, and the three soul mates found their way to the hidden valley Joseph had found two days before. While Jack and Sadie drank from the pool below the spring Joseph found a patch of wild strawberries. It soon become apparent to Joseph that both Jack's and Sadie's appetites were not limited to their customary foods. Time soon passed, and it was time to bring the goats back to the corral.

Jack expected the boy to stop at the corral gate and send him to bring in the goats. He was a little puzzled at first when the boy guided the horse to a rise overlooking the goats. There the boy leaned forward; raising his hand high in the air, he signaled with a long, sweeping motion toward the goat corral.

From the hilltop, Joseph imagined himself a fierce Indian chief directing his warriors into battle with raiding warriors of a rival Indian nation. Jack being his only warrior and the goats his defenseless adversaries mattered little; deep within his sub-consciousness he became one with his ancestors.

Jack had understood the boy's signal and soon had the goats headed toward the corral. At the same time, he was looking for the Great Pyrenees dogs. Then before he realized it, they were beside him. Jack wondered how they concealed themselves so well, and more important why they did not bring the goats in themselves.

He watched as the magnificent dogs followed the goats into their corral. He could not understand the Great Pyrenees living with a goat herd. They were canines like him—how could they humble themselves?

It was late afternoon when Joseph had finishing his chores. He took special care to brush and care for Silver Star. What of his sister? What had he done to cause her to treat him differently? If that was what she wanted then he would go along with her. He knew she still needed him, and he would always watch out for her.

That evening Ida Belle was not sitting at the table but was in the kitchen with her mother. The time of the cutting horse contest was coming soon, and his older brother was asking if Joseph would help with preparation. Joseph missed seeing Ida Belle across the table and was distracted when she served the meal. His attention returned to the conversation just as his father said it was a good idea especially if Joseph might have to take his place.

Joseph was still thinking about how he would find time to help his brothers when he came into his great-grandmother's room. He was glad to see his sister already there. Maybe he did think both his sister and great-grandmother were a little peculiar, but in a good way. What would his great-grandmother tell them today?

It was a while before Warmwind began to speak. "It is time for me to talk of the time of great indecision—a time of choice, that of remaining warriors, becoming land owners, and moving to lands called reservations. The choice of your forefather is your heritage today, although I believe you would have chosen differently.

"I have told you of our journey to the land of the vapors; but I had not told you our village and hunting grounds had become part of the United States in something called the Louisiana Purchase. In the eyes of the government in the east, the Wazhazhe nation owned most of the land between the Missouri and Arkansas Rivers.

"There had been much discussion among the leaders in council lodges all over the Wazhazhe Nation; it was not our choice to become landowners. It was agreed to sell fifty million acres to the federal government. The settlers from the east had pressed the eastern Indian tribes into that land, upsetting the hunting grounds.

"There were those of our clan who spoke at the council meetings of a time when the land would no longer be rich in wildlife, native fruits, and plants. To save their land they must learn the ways of the foreigners of the east and learn to farm and ranch. Others believed they should rid the lands

of the invaders and let the land return to its natural harmony like it was before the invaders came.

"One morning Whitedeer could not be found; I was called to the council lodge in her place. It was a strange feeling to sit in the place of Whitedeer. I could feel the amethyst stone turn warm; it was as though Whitedeer were with me still.

"The leaders of the council agreed it was a matter of those choosing to keep the old ways and those willing to learn the ways of the farmers and ranchers."

Joseph could not hold back his curiosity and asked his great-grandmother if that was when the family settled on the ranch. Warmwind said no—she would will tell them more another day; now it was getting late, and could they continue the next day?

CHAPTER TWENTY-TWO:

THE PROMISE

Joseph had once again eaten his breakfast early on and was out moving the goats into the open field near the newly built goat pens and shelter; it would be the last time he would need to release the goats from the corral.

The goat herd had become familiar with the land and its mountain terrain. They had become much better at choosing the best sites to forage than he could. The mornings were now his to wander the land with his two companions.

It was not by accident they found themselves waiting near the rock formation where they lost track of the three goats before. Suddenly the goats appeared and then disappeared. Joseph and his dog were completely baffled. There was no way to escape past them, and they could not have climbed the high cliffs of the rock formation.

Sadie had only an accommodating interest in their pursuit and decided to search out the aroma of fresh tree blossoms. Along one side of the rock foundation she discovered what she had been looking for. The tree was full of blooms growing up the side of the rock formation.

She had just stripped a small branch full of blooms when a whiff of goat contaminated the aroma of the blossoms. The three goats had been watching from their hiding place in the passageway that led to an isolated area within the rock formation. Not wanting to be discovered, the three goats raced out from the opening and underneath Sadie.

Sadie bolted back, snorting her displeasure. Both Joseph and Jack came to see what was happening just in time to see the goats disappear into the brush.

Sadie could sense the perplexed emotions of her two companions, but after giving casual consideration to her duty directed her attentions back to the tree blossoms; their uneasiness did not have anything to do with her or the passageway behind the tree anyway.

Jack searched for their scent, unable to backtrack to where the goat came from because of the fragrant smell of the blossoms. After a while Jack and Joseph tired of the chase; it was a hot day, a very good day to go swimming.

Joseph remembered the hidden canyon that opened up into a valley concealed by high cliffs and tall tree formations. There was a waterfall where the stream flowed down the smooth rock face; it formed a perfect water slide. Joseph only had to pat the hips of his Indian pony for Jack to jump up behind him.

Sadie especially liked to race through the rough terrain. Once she understood where the boy wanted her to go he left it up to her to make her own way there. She did not like being alone, and Silver Star was too slow. With both the boy and dog with her she did not have to be by herself, and their added weight made the jumps and turns more challenging.

It was not long before the trio entered the secluded valley. The waterfall was everything Joseph remembered. Joseph could see it was not an easy climb up to a ledge that joined to the waterfall. As he climbed, Jack barked a warning to be careful, thinking, What is the kid doing now? *Joseph's first trip down the waterfall met with astonished cries from his two companions. Jack pulled the boy out of the water by his leather buckskins.*

When Joseph began to climb once more, Jack knew he would fall once more. This time Jack left him in the water. It was during Joseph's third trip down the falls that Jack knew he was not falling and it must be something good to do. On his fourth trip down the waterfall Joseph had not come out of the water when Jack came down the slide after him.

Jack was not going to let the boy outdo him. It was a race to see who could reach the ledge first. Sadie had watched the spectacle with some reservations. She was still warm from the run she had just finished. At first she just stomped the water, letting the water splash on to her.

Before long Sadie was galloping through the stream with the water and mud spattering all the way over her back. At one part of the stream the mud was too enticing to resist, and she began to roll over to one side and then the other. When she returned to the waterfall the only part of her body without mud was around her eyes.

Joseph began to laugh until he realized unless he got the mud off her he would have a slippery ride back to the goats. On the bank of the stream Jack found a warm spot where he could watch the boy, his attention divided between the boy and the goat herd—had they returned to the corral just as Joseph had planned?

Ida Belle was at the doorway to Warmwind's room when Joseph had finished eating and listening to the family news. She whispered to Joseph, "Warmwind was feeling very weak—she may be asleep. Maybe we should not go in." She opened her door and looked in, only to find her great-grandmother sitting on the rug facing the window.

Warmwind did not wait till Joseph and Ida Belle had reached her before she began. "The time is getting near for my departure. You will need to know about my most trying times, the reservations, and my return to the Ouachita Mountains.

"You have not forgotten to discover the mystery of Whitedeer and the clan's sacred bundles. You must promise; and remember the past and the present they are one."

Ida Belle said, *"We promise."*

"You must promise too, Joseph," Warmwind whispered when their eyes met.

"I promise," Joseph answered, *thinking,* I will keep the promise even if I do not know exactly how the past and present can be one.

"Great-grandmother," he asked, *"if you tell us more about the sacred objects we are searching for we can find them faster; and it would help if we knew what part of the past would be one with the present."*

"Let's see," Warmwind began, *"our clan's bundles were like most other clans' bundles. It's been so long maybe there may not be much left to recognize. Look for the remains of a woven buffalo skin bag, inside a deerskin bag, and inside that a woven mat bag. You will know you found it if the remains of hawk are within.*

"The pipe is almost the same as the one still in the small closet in the corner of the tack room. That should not have changed that much."

Ida Belle spoke up, saying, *"Tell us more about the sacred bundles."*

Warmwind replied, *"You must give me time to remember.*

"I do remember that when a war party left the village, the leader always carried one of the clan bundles. You must understand for the braves going into battle the bundle symbolized their strength and courage. The most sacred part was the special war club and the wrap in which the hawk was placed."

Joseph wanted to hear more about the war club. He could imagine he was one of the braves going into battle, but what was symbolic about a wrap? The hawk was different; he understood about the hawk. Anyone who had watched a hawk in flight or in battle could see a brave would want to imitate it.

Warmwind returned to her rocking chair and slowly began to rock, her mind venturing back into the past. Ida Belle asked Great-grandmother, "Where have the spirits taken you?"

Warmwind said, "It is as if it was only yesterday our clan elders had decided to move our village from this valley. The federal government through a series of treaties had given title to lands west of our village to the Indian tribes across the great river.

"Our village would be impractical to defend against renegade war parties with the aid of their allies. There was much discussion and deliberation in the council lodge. I had once again been seated in the place of Whitedeer.

"It was difficult for me to concentrate; I was mindful of a young warrior, called Lone Eagle, a little older than myself.

"A vision began to appear within my thoughts. I was on a high mountain, or hill, looking out over the surrounding lands below. There were two rivers some distance away, one to the west the other to the east. There were deer grazing in the meadows and lush fields of plants and fruit. The vision disappeared when the young warrior became aware my attention was upon him.

"All discussions stopped, and the elders ended the meeting asking the young warrior to join them. The next day the young warrior was sent to scout the land in my vision. I had asked my grandfather why he was called Lone Eagle and why had he gone alone.

"He answered, 'Not many years ago, because of his speed and ability to see great distances, he was sent with a government agent to explore the rivers within our lands. He is like the lone eagle flying high in the sky, seeing everything and always searching for the next mountain, river, or valley to explore. It would only slow him down to have sent other with him.'

"Within a week Lone Eagle had returned; he reported the hill and surrounding terrain suitable for defense, hunting, and trapping. The two rivers allowed transportation north to the trading post or south to other villages.

"On the day before we began our journey to the new village, Whitedeer was seen at the cave below the council lodge but she then instantaneously disappeared. Whitedeer and the sacred object hidden inside the cave were missing. The whole village searched for her through the night."

Warmwind, seeing Ida Belle's questioning look, interrupted her story and said, "The amethyst stone had remained cold and without color.

"The next day our scouts reported seeing a large war party coming over the mountains to the east. The fate of Whitedeer was put aside, and we moved the village that night.

"We traveled northwest each day until we reached the Neosho and Verdigris river inlets into the Arkansas River. The village camped for three days while the scouts went out in all directions.

"On the fourth day we traveled north between the two rivers to the land of my vision. It was a land that permitted our tribe to continue their natural ways of hunting and trapping, even though all in the village knew it was not as before. Each day our scouts brought news from other villages and the tribal councils of the big and little Wazhazhe nation.

"One day news was brought of the massacre of a Wazhazhe village in the south by depraved renegade warriors and their allies. It was then my grandfather called me to his lodge telling me I must marry. It was not a surprise; the ways of our tribe were coming to an end. But who would I marry?

"All the braves that were unmarried were troubled by the difficulties I may pose to such a marriage, except one: Lone Eagle. We married that afternoon.

"The days passed quickly, Lone Eagle journeying throughout the land to bring news to our village while I remained serving on the council. One day

Lone Eagle returned from the north; he told of missionary schools teaching French and the English studies to Indian children.

"It was then my youngest sister was chosen to leave the village and learn of the English ways. Each summer she would return to teach me of the school and of their ways. Soon I was translating both the French and English words for the council. It was also the year Lone Eagle was sent on a venture east of the great river and the twins, both boys, were born.

"Ten years had passed, and many had left our village; the wildlife was no longer abundant, and the land once held by the Wazhazhe Nation was by treaties sold to another Indian nation. I had given Lone Eagle another son and two daughters by then."

Warmwind had only to pause when Joseph asked her, to tell them more about Lone Eagle. It was the first time anyone had talked about their great-grandfather. "You said our great-grandfather was an explorer and a scout; was he a great warrior and a chief? There was a picture of you when you were young; is there one of him?"

Warmwind said, "He fought when he had to; he was a scout. That is all that mattered." Warmwind once more went off into her own thoughts, and the twins without a sound left her room.

Joseph, allowing his mind to wander, could imagine his great-grandfather on a scouting mission—probably in search of buffalo or of a hostile war party. He let his mind search out every feature of his gear, his clothes, and the special way he had decorated his horse. It was then he became conscious of Ida Belle beside him.

As Ida Belle left him she smiled, whispering, *"Of course the horse would look like Sadie."*

Chapter Twenty-three:

Traditions sweep away "customs and rituals"

Ida Belle was in the kitchen before her mother the next morning. She had been unable to sleep most of the night thinking about the promise she had made to her great-grandmother. Was there a reason why Whitedeer had not revealed her fate and that of the clan's sacred bundles to her great-grandmother?

It was within Ida Belle's power to know of such things, but the reason eluded her. Was it not as simple as counting the fingers on her hand? From her first thoughts had she not welcomed the gifts of the ancients? She had searched the voice and watched the eyes of her great-grandmother; the answer was not there.

Joseph had also been preoccupied with the promise he had made to his great-grandmother. When he and his two comrades came in sight of the new livestock corrals, the goat herd was already at the gate ready to be let out. It was not long before the goat herd began to graze in a field some distance away.

After the big storm two new corrals were built on opposite sides of a large building with pens, stalls, and storage rooms. At the back of the building an arena with connected pens was set aside for training horses; Joseph could see his two brothers bringing cattle of all sizes into the arena.

Last night he had heard his oldest brother Alvin had failed the medical examination because of poor eyesight and would not be going into the war. No one was happier than Joseph; deep within him was the knowledge that his brother was not a warrior and would not have returned from combat.

In some way he felt the need to protect his older brothers; he did not know why. They were older, considerably more skilled and knowledgeable of farming and ranching

Once everything was in place, Alvin explained they would be separating the cows into three groups. Joseph was to open the gate of one of three pens depending on age of the cow they had cut out of the herd. He was to keep track of how long it took for Alvin and then Ruben to have all the cows in the assigned pens.

It all seemed simple enough to Joseph, except he knew Rubin would have the advantage when it came his turn because the cows would know which pen to go into.

When it came time for Rubin, Joseph switched pen assignments for the different ages. Joseph thought his brothers and their horses were competing well, but he believed Sadie could do a better job than either horse. It was then he noticed both Sadie and Jack looking on from outside the arena.

After his brothers had finished their exercise they said he had done well and they would see him at the stables later. Joseph watched them as they left to return the cattle to the main herd. It was time to close the goat herd up for the night. Joseph had to hold Sadie back from helping as Jack drove the goats into the corral. Okay, Sadie, *he thought,* maybe tomorrow my brothers will not be using the arena.

That evening Warmwind expressed only a slight interest in the activities of the ranch and began to tell the twins of the reservations. "Many years passed, and my oldest sons were in their nineteenth year. One would go with their father while the other remained behind with the rest of the family. It was clear to see they had learned much from their travels with their father.

"It was the year a treaty was signed, moving our village and those villages to the south to a land only a short distance to the north. The treaty promised in exchange instructions on ranching and farming, along with the animals and equipment needed.

"There were passionate debates at the council lodge, where each clan voiced their opinions. Lone Eagle said nothing; he had long ago anticipated the events that overwhelmed the village.

"It was not so with my older sons, one for going to the reservation and learning the ways of a rancher, while the other was opposed, discouraging others from giving up their traditional ways. It was the second time the spirits of our ancestors abandoned me. The village became divided into two groups. I was divided in my thoughts and could no longer give guidance to the council.

"Our days on the reservation were difficult, with one son learning the ways of ranching even as his brother joined other warriors in fighting the enemies of the Wazhazhe. Life became more increasingly difficult as game was driven further away as the settlers moved westward.

"The leaders of our village discouraged those who wished to farm and traded the livestock and equipment for goods. One leader who sided with those who wanted to farm was threatened with removal as chief.

"Lone Eagle along with his two youngest sons had built up a thriving business trading pelts and furs in exchange for merchandise that they used to barter with the tribes of the prairies for more pelts and furs.

"*Although the profits were considerable, he longed to live away from the turbulence and confusion of the reservation.*"

Warmwind had become weak from speaking and said she would talk of their return to Ouachita Mountains when she was not so faint. After leaving their great-grandmother's room, Joseph tried to start a conversation with his sister only to find she had disappeared into her room. He wanted to know what she knew about their promise. It was probably just as well.

Joseph could feel the excitement in both Jack and Sadie the next morning as they joined Alvin and Rubin at the barn arena. Jack knew at once there were bad-tempered cows in this arena.

If given the opportunity he would have taken control of the small herd; instead, he could only watch from outside the arena. Each time the boy stepped into the arena Jack gave out a deep, threatening growl as a warning to the cows they would have to answer to him.

Joseph had heard his cattle dog. It was an impossible situation for him; he could not put down his older brothers by revealing his uncertainty in their abilities to handle the problem. He was sure they were not aware of the danger they were in.

This day Alvin and Rubin took turns cutting out one cow after another until only five enraged cows remained. Alvin had just selected one cow when another charged, knocking his horse to the ground with him pinned beneath.

Even though Jack had been commanded to stay out of the arena, he leaped onto some seats and over the fence, charging first one cow then another, driving the other cows away from Alvin and his fallen horse.

C.R. Redcorn

No matter which way the cows turned, Jack was there nipping an ear, a nose, or the hoof intended to crush him or send him flying. In a short time the cows had given up and retreated to one side of the arena.

Joseph opened a gate to an empty pen; Jack drove the cows into the pen, making sure the offending cow received a sting she would remember. He had learned how to deliver a painful bite without permanently hurting his adversary.

With the cows secure in the pen Joseph and Rubin pulled Alvin out from beneath the injured horse. From nowhere Ida Belle was there asking

Rubin to harness a horse to the buckboard and giving Joseph instructions of what she needed to help Alvin. With Alvin safely in the buckboard, Joseph rode to get the doctor.

It was a serious event for the family; not only was Alvin hurt with an injured leg and bruised ribs; their chance for winning the contest was in jeopardy. All had given up on their best cutting horse. After Jack, Joseph and Sadie moved the cows from the arena and back to the main herd, Ida Belle began to care for the injured horse.

The next day Joseph proudly looked on as his dog was praised by each and every one and elevated to a place of honor within the community. Jack could only wonder what was so important—was he not just doing his job?

Humans are strange, *he pondered;* they recognize a difference of individualism and heroism among themselves but do not understand it is also part of the animal world too.

After sending the goats off to pasture, Joseph set aside all of his everyday jobs and returned to the tack room to work on his totem. Just as before, to his astonishment the wood seemed to fly off the post on its own. Before long he had finished his second totem.

This time he had noticed his sister standing between Jack and Sadie outside the tack room. He was sure she had influenced his work in some way but could not be completely sure.

Chapter Twenty-four:

Cultural heredity

Ida Belle had moved quietly into Warmwind's room that evening after the evening meal, not wanting to be noticed by Joseph. It was not by accident that she had come to the arena. An overwhelming presence had swept over her; what power or spirit had called her to the arena to the aid of her brother and the horse?

Warmwind asked Ida Belle to tell her what was troubling her.

Ida Belle answered, "It is the power or spirit that empowers awareness beyond my imagination."

Warmwind replied that the energies of the other worlds take on many forms and various means of conveying perception.

Ida Belle could hear Joseph coming up the stairs and quickly asked one more question. "I believe there is another that is cleverer than I who knows of the other worlds—would that be Joseph?"

Warmwind started to answer, saying, "Yes, it is as it you suspect, although—" but was interrupted as Joseph came into the room.

Ida Belle observed Joseph cautiously as he entered the room. Well, if this is the path he has chosen so be it. She could also amuse herself with the deception; although in all the years before why had she not caught him?

171

Joseph, seeing his sister's attention on him breathed a sigh of relief. Maybe they would become close again like before.

Warmwind could only manage a very small smile, deciding it would be better to let the perplexity continue. To begin, she said, "The dog Jack is of great importance. Please tell me all about his rescue of Alvin."

Joseph, being very proud of his dog, gave his version of the incident at the arena.

Ida Belle thought, He is not telling everything; he is very cagey. *It must have been him who appealed to her to come to the arena. If that was so, then why did he need her; could he not have controlled the cow before she charged? She had been so deep in thought she did not hear her great-grandmother begin to talk about her return to the Ouachita Mountains.*

Warmwind raised her voice, saying, "One day my husband left the village alone without our two youngest sons, without a word to anyone. Upon his return five days later he pronounced he was taking his family back to the Ouachita Mountains. To his two oldest sons, he would leave the decision to come or stay for them to decide."

"With the profits from his business he had purchased two thousand acres of land along the Washita Mountain Range; we would clear the land and began ranching.

"We said farewell to the clan and to one son who chose to stay on the reservation and continue to fight the enemies of the Wazhazhe Nation.

"Before leaving we were joined by the families of my sister and those of three cousins. The fireplaces of our clan that once numbered in the hundreds now were less than twenty. It was then I understood the ways of Wazhazhe, our ancestors, were passing before us."

Ida Belle anxiously asked, "Were there not those who still followed the traditions of the Wazhazhe?"

Warmwind answered, "Yes, but only the most gifted who could walk in the shadows of Wakonta while silently providing favor to those around them."

Ida Belle understood but asked her great-grandmother, "Why could those close to the ones who possessed the gifts of the ancients not recognize their presence?"

To this Warmwind nodded her head and said, "Yes, but you must remember that while they continued living in the shadows of Wakonda others were giving up the ways of the Wazhazhe. Unfortunately there were those, like myself, who gradually lost their ability to recognize the subtle behavior of nature's energies."

Joseph, wanting to hear more about his great-grandmother's return to the Ouachita Mountains, said, "Tell us more, especially about leaving the reservation?"

Warmwind continued her account of the trip back to the Ouachita Mountains. "It was a long journey as we headed east crossing rugged lands and rushing rivers to avoid tribes hostile to the Wazhazhe. We traveled on east until we reached the White River, where Lone Eagle had made arrangements to met with the family of my sister, Willow."

"It was a wonderful reunion meeting all the children of Willow. They were more like the settlers than Wazhazhe or Kansa. They no longer built their fireplaces as one and lived together under one lodge. What was the most troubling was that they no longer followed the ritual in which the name of one of the clan's life symbols was given to their children. Was that to be our destiny?

"Two days later we headed southwest along the White River, passing through the site of our old village and on to the Buffalo River, were we camped for a day. The following day we reach the edge of the Washita Mountain Range, where we camped for two days; the mountain trails were not safe, and we would have to travel later on a little-known trail.

"It was on our last night that I lost the amethyst stone in the mountains above the council lodge. It was late in the day, and the others had continued on to the medicine lodge below."

Ida Belle let the words of her great-grandmother float back in her subliminal consciousness, turning her thoughts to Joseph.

Was it not improbable that he could find the amethyst stone after all that time? Is it not possible the visions that came to me through his voice and reasoning were of his energy, not mine? Is it not true there is always an uncertainty in what is, and rarely the disbelief in what is not?

For Joseph, the words of his great-grandmother would possibly provide a solution to the pledge he had made. His promise was somewhat of an inconvenience—what good could come from discovering what had happened to Whitedeer?

He was well aware of the change in Ida Belle's behavior toward him; it was not easy to understand what caused a girl to do what she did. It was important for Ida Belle and his great-grandmother to discover what happened to Whitedeer, and that was enough for him.

Warmwind had begun to talk of their first days on their native soil. How they first camped around the council lodge and began to clear the land. Lone Eagle kept watch, provided the game, and most often could be found on a mountain cliff or hilltop looking out over horizon.

She knew his heart was not in the ranch; the call of the distant lands beyond the mountains and plains beckoned to the adventurous spirit within him. It was more as though in some way he was destined to wander in search of that which was known only to him.

Joseph closed his eyes, and images of his great-grandfather began to fill his mind; visions of his ancestral clan's life symbols of long ago replaced those of the glorified warriors he had once revered.

He was filled with happiness and then sadness; he had found his place in life but became aware he could be the last Sho-Kah spiritual descendant of the "messenger" clan.

Both Joseph and Ida Belle had not noticed that their great-grandmother had stopped speaking, Ida Belle concentrating on Joseph while Joseph remained occupied in sorting out his situation. He must know more about his ancestors, the Sho-Kah clan.

But first he would have to solve the mystery of Whitedeer. Ida Belle sensed Joseph was deeply involved in some sort of dilemma; she believed he would now reveal his true nature.

It was not to be; Joseph regained his composure when Warmwind continued telling the twins about the ranch. "Within five years a meadow was cleared of brush and trees, an orchard started, and we were growing vegetables in our gardens. It was then our first neighbors arrived in the valley—some to farm and some to ranch, while others came to prospect for minerals.

"It was not at all like it is today. The terrain was rugged with only animal trails leading into and out of our valley. It was the miners who first came to our camp for help with their ills and sickness, then other followed. They in turn helped us learn the settler's ways of ranching and farming. The young of our family gave up many of the ways of our ancestors building houses, stables, and barns.

"One summer day Lone Eagle looked upon me, and I understood we would be returning to our people on the land called Osage. You must understand clan membership was of great importance to us; we were Wazhazhe by virtue of our membership in a clan. Lone Eagle was needed to resume his place as official messenger, 'Sho-kah' of the clan.

"You must know that I will be returning to the reservation soon." With a great sigh she said, "My time is growing short, and I have finished what I must."

Joseph and Ida Belle left their great-grandmother's room uncertain what to do next.

They could not be sure of what she had just told them, each with their own thoughts and interpretation. What was unmistakable to both was that to keep their promise they would have to find out what happened to Whitedeer soon.

As they walked down the stairs without talking it was understood they must proceed together. The last place Whitedeer was seen was the ceremonial cave. It was there they must find the answer.

Sarah stopped reading. "That's it," she whispered, once more closing her eyes and letting her thoughts wander, searching her mind.

Sarah's heart almost stopped when she heard, "Were you looking for me?"

Sarah opened her eyes, saying, "Hanna are you really here?"

Hanna could not keep from laughing, saying, "Of course I am, silly—I am behind you."

Hanna, seeing Sarah's disappointment, continued. "Please understand the gift; you must think in the ways of our Indian ancestors. The images, they convey a different meaning in the minds of those not Wazhazhe."

Sarah thought, *Then why am I here reading this journal, and why does the journal seem to be conversing with me if I am not thinking Wazhazhe?* She remembered the day she first came into the Ouachita Mountains.

Was it her desire to know of her ancestors that had brought this journal to her? There were many questions flashing through her mind. What part did she have to play in the promise to Warmwind?

Chapter Twenty-five:

Searching for
the Lost Sacred Objects

All the rest of that day and that night Sarah could not dismiss the feeling she must somehow help Joseph and Ida Belle find the missing sacred bundles and find out what had happened to Whitedeer. But how could she? Even if it were possible for the ancients to visit the present in dreams, how could she visit her ancestors in the past?

Warmwind talked of the purest form of Nature's energies like a medium for sending thoughts and knowledge to others. Could that be like the sun's rays were a medium for sight? Or maybe it was like the instincts found in animals that help them live their lives. It was all very confusing.

What was it Jack the dog had thought about the trickster? The imaginary, elusive trickster had the ability to defy both time and space; humans had long ago lost their understanding of the supernatural world where the trickster resided. It all did not make sense to her, a supernatural world and who or what was the trickster. *And now I am citing what a dog was thinking.*

In an instant she realized that if it was that true long ago humans, animals, and other living things lived in a world where they in some way communicated with each other and became conscious of a natural energy in nature, maybe the medium she was looking for was the supernatural world of the trickster. It was clear that whoever wrote the journal walked in the shadows of such a world.

The question was who had written the journal, and for whom was it written? It was very real and was not written for Joseph or Ida Belle. In her search for answers, Sarah had eliminated Joseph, Ida Belle, and Warmwind as the ones who wrote the journal; not that they could not have written it, but she could not help feeling the one who wrote the journal was most clever and really gifted.

Sarah once again questioned if it was all real or a very clever prank being played on her. It was almost like a game of charade; in either case she had only a short time left to solve the dilemma before going back home and to school. She would begin by searching for clues in the cave below the stables, and maybe she could find out if it was all real or not.

On her way back to the stables Sarah remembered the rock formation where the three goats had hidden from Joseph and his dog Jack. If the journal was written for her, whoever had written the journal obviously intended for her to search for the rock formation and find out what was there. Maybe she would, but only when she knew it was not just more mischief. *Where is Hanna?*

Then it occurred to her: if it was a clever trick, would the ones playing the trick not watch to see if she searched for the hidden rock formation? Yes, tomorrow she would visit the cave and put an end to their tricks. There was a problem, though; in some way she knew it was not trickery or her cousin's mischief.

The next day Sarah spent the morning investigating the cave for any clue to what might have happened to Whitedeer. She was just about to give up, when from the entranceway to the cave she could see a rock formation in the distance. Sarah was trying to decide if it could be the same one written about in the journal when she heard the thin whistle "pe-heeeeeeee" of a large, stocky eagle circling overhead.

The eagle landed in a tree only a few feet away from Sarah. "Sarah, do not be frightened—it is I, Hanna."

"You are the eagle?" Sarah called out.

"No, silly I am standing beside you," answered Hanna. "The eagle, it is not dangerous—can you not see that?"

The eagle circled above Sarah and once more returned to the tree above her, this time chirping a gentle but subtle "cutta-cutta-cutta-cutta"—an invitation for her to follow. Sarah no longer had any doubts that Joseph, Ida Belle, and the journal were not real and together with Hanna rode after the eagle.

The eagle flew past the old livestock corrals and barns on to a rock formation surrounded by a deep thicket of trees and brush. Sarah remembered that there was only one tree at the rock formation in the journal. Was this the right rock formation, and how could she find the passageway that led to the secluded area within the rocks?

Sarah searched the walls of the rock formation without success until she noticed the eagle hovering over a tree with branches obscuring a large section of the rock formation. The eagle landed on a branch of the tree and gave the familiar gentle chirp Sarah recognized as an appeal for her to follow.

From the trunk of the tree Sarah could see a ledge just a few feet over her head. By climbing the tree and walking across a limb she was able to reach the ledge. From the ledge Sarah could see there was a passageway leading through the rock formation into a large cavern opening to the sky just like in Warmwind's dream.

"Hurry," Sarah called to Hanna, helping her up the tree and across the limb. The passageway was dark, but Sarah could see there were drawings of all kinds on the walls: some of animals, others that must be telling a story of native Indian life.

At the end of the passageway Sarah could see within an open area rocks arranged in a fashion that reminded her of a classroom or a place of worship. There were three natural caverns going back into the rock formation, each with a different depiction of ancient lifestyles painted on each side of the entrance.

Sarah began to study the drawings, trying to understand their meaning, and had not noticed the thunderstorm beginning to form in the sky above. The sky grew dark, and across the sky lightning and thunder signaled the approaching downpour of rain that sent Sarah and Hanna into the closest cavern.

Inside the cavern there were more drawings similar to those at the passageway. As Sarah ventured farther back in the cavern the light became so dim it was difficult see the faded drawings clearly.

With each lightning strike the figures on the wall became more defined and took on a lifelike appearance. Sarah became frightened and ran from the cavern only to have the rain drive her back into a second cavern.

In this cavern she found more drawings, but this time they appeared to be from a time more recent than those in first cave. This time when the lightning came Sarah was not frightened.

Sarah noticed this cavern was better formed, with three definite walls, the back wall and two side walls each with drawings that were different from the others. Sarah was excited about what she had discovered but thought, *What of Whitedeer?* There was no evidence of Whitedeer or that any clan's sacred bundles were here; she would look in the last cavern.

This next cavern was even better formed, with drawings on both sides and shelves cut into the back wall. On the shelves Sarah found one pipe and what must have been the clan's missing sacred bundles.

Sarah thought there must be more, some other reason why Whitedeer brought the clan's sacred bundles here. Whitedeer must have been painting the walls of the caverns for many years; but why did she leave the sacred objects, and what happened to her?

Sarah revisited the first two caverns and found the drawings were of three different styles, maybe by different artists at different times. The lightning had stopped, and the figures on the walls no longer gave the appearance of being lifelike.

Sarah considered taking some of the clan's sacred bundles back to the council lodge but Hanna by only lowering her eyes persuaded her otherwise.

Sarah suddenly became conscious that her grandfather and the cousins would be worried about her caught out in the lightening storm. Also she had forgotten all about Misty waiting outside the rock formation for her.

She waited only until the thunder and lightning had quieted down before leaving the rock formation. Misty was waiting in a growth of trees not far away and gave out an impatient whinny as if to say, *Hurry up—it's wet out here.*

On her ride back to the ranch house Sarah realized that she must in some way let her grandfather know all that she had experienced since coming to the ranch; was he not a messenger and Sho-Kah?

And yes, she would fulfill all that was expected of her, whatever that would be, as she followed in the footsteps of Ida Belle and her ancestors.

Her thoughts turned to her great-grandfather Joseph; could she be the most recent spiritual descendant of the Sho-Kah "messenger" clan? And what of Ida Belle—had she become a gifted one, and was there possibly another that followed her? The journal had not revealed much about all this.

Two days passed before Sarah could get away and once more find time to return to the journal. She was anxious to find out if Joseph and Ida Belle had discovered the caverns hidden away in the rock formation. It probably would be more difficult since Ida Belle had returned the amethyst stone back to Warmwind.

Part Six:

UNRAVELING THE MYSTERY

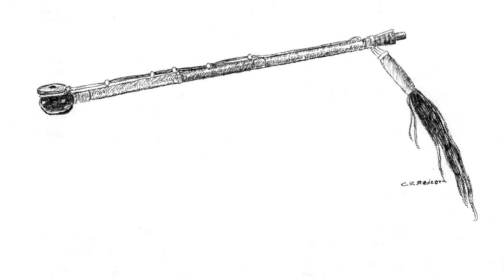

Chapter Twenty-six:

The caverns: "the senses"

Ida Belle was up very early the next morning; she had not slept well that night as she questioned if she ever had the ability to foresee her brother's thoughts and visualize what he experienced. In her mind it was such a mysterious talent she wondered if it was her brother's gift and not hers.

Warmwind had confirmed the presence of one much more clever and gifted than she but did not actually say who it was; it must be Joseph. No matter; she had made a promise to her great-grandmother, and that was more important. This afternoon she would return to the cave and begin searching for any clues of what happened to Whitedeer.

Joseph hardly looked his sister's way when he came down for breakfast; he would help her search for what happened to Whitedeer and the other things. Although the pipe and the war club did interest him, taking care of the goat herd and helping prepare for the cutting horse competition would have to come first.

This day he would be riding his older brother's favorite cutting horse, Nellie, for the first time. He had seen his older brother work the cattle; his horse was very fast and moved well.

Both Jack and Sadie were waiting for Joseph when he reached the stables. Both noticed a change in the boy, but that was common in humans and to be expected. Jack could sense Sadie was not comfortable with the way the boy went about his tasks while not giving much attention to her. It was of little consequence; it only reminded him that it was the responsibility of canines, like him, to provide a balance between humans and the rest of the animal kingdom.

Soon the goat herd was quietly grazing in a nearby valley without incident; the three mischievous goats had slipped off earlier. On the way back to the stables Sadie had the inclination to stop over at a nearby thicket of trees.

The persimmons were getting sweet, and they were one of her favorite treats. At first Joseph urged her to continue on to the stables, but it soon became evident that both Jack and Sadie were of the same way of thinking. Joseph gave in and was soon filling himself with the best persimmons.

It was just after noon when Joseph had rounded up the equipment necessary to begin his exercises for the cutting horse competition that was only days away. How could his life have changed so much? He longed to return to the days when he had few little obligations and could roam the ranch as he pleased.

If Rubin was called into the army he would have to compete in the cutting horse competition. How many times had he heard the family talk about how the prize money would make everything easier?

Alvin and Rubin were waiting at the cattle barn arena when Joseph, Jack, and Sadie arrived. It did not take much imagination to tell that they were just as concerned about the upcoming contest as Joseph was. Together they made plans first for Rubin to work the cattle then for Joseph to work the cattle with Alvin's horse.

Alvin gave encouragement and advice as Rubin went through his group of cows in record time. Jack watched from one of the bleacher seats, unable to understand why they used horses when he was there; could he not have driven the cows into the corrals much faster and without all the fuss?

Sadie on the other hand watched with some amusement. She could see no reason for moving the cows from one totally empty corral to another even smaller corral. The only reason she watched was because the boy was involved. Her enjoyment ended when the boy began to ride another horse called Nellie; that mare had never, ever thought for herself.

Sadie had seen the man who most often rode Nellie fall off and be hurt by an angry cow. The boy could be hurt too, seeing how irresponsible that mare was.

It soon became evident to all that it was not working. The horse was waiting for Alvin's commands before taking charge of cutting out a cow and moving it to a different corral. Sadie anxiously stood by knowing that the boy was having trouble; she could not help him.

After a while, with Alvin's help and encouragement, Joseph was able to learn the commands that the horse could understand and follow. It was not exactly what Joseph considered practical. It was getting late in the day when it was agreed they would try again tomorrow.

Ida Belle had been struggling that morning with her chores when her mother asked her if there was something she needed to attend too. There was; she had promised to find something for Great-grandmother. It did not take her long to saddle Silver Star, ride to the cave, and begin searching for any clue of Whitedeer or the sacred objects.

After some time Ida Belle thought, How foolish; this cave has been searched so many times before, *If only she had kept the amethyst stone, maybe it would have revealed some clue.*

On her way out of the cave a feeling of not being alone came upon her. Closing her eyes, the image of the rock formation and the three goats appeared in her thoughts. To her disbelief the rock formation she had just visualized was there, almost hidden within the tree line some distance away.

Ida Belle had just mounted her horse when she caught sight of Joseph on his way to bring in the goat herd. In her excitement she forgot all about her suspicions and raced down to meet him. Joseph had never seen his sister so excited, and after hearing of her premonition told her of the three goats and of their disappearance around that rock formation.

On their way to the rock formation Ida Belle began to have doubts if Joseph was the one her great-grandmother was talking about being more clever than herself. Had she not been aware of the difficulty he was experiencing while training for the cutting horse competition? Why had he not found the passageway she had visualized? No! It was not Joseph, but then who was it?

It took Ida Belle only a short time before she found the passageway leading to an open area in the center of the rock formation. Even Jack was mystified when she climbed into the tree branches and disappeared, although he was first to follow. Then Joseph came, after making sure Sadie and Silver Star were free to wander about.

Joseph found Ida Belle standing before an entrance to one of three natural caverns enclosed within walls of the rock formation; she was staring at a village scene painted on the rock wall. The paint was washed-out and faded, almost worn away by the wind and rains.

He watched as she began to sway back and forth, speaking in a way he did not understand. "Joseph," she cried out, "can you see it?"

Joseph at first could not, saying, "What is it I should see?"

"Do you not remember the dream of the village and of the woman that waved to you? It was not a gift from Great-grandmother; it was a gift from the one called Whitedeer."

"Yes, it is true" Joseph answered. "The village in this drawing is like the one in his dream." Still what his sister was asking him to consider was a little foolish. The one called Whitedeer died years ago; how could she have waved to him, especially in a dream?

Joseph followed Ida Belle into the cavern, where they found more drawings similar to the one at the cavern entrance. The drawings were very old, containing pictures and symbols they did not recognize. Still they looked for signs that would tell them what had happened to Whitedeer and the sacred bundles. After a while they were satisfied there was not any sign of Whitedeer, going on to the next cavern.

Jack had returned when Joseph and Ida Belle were entering the second cavern. If the boy could enter the caverns so could he—had he not left only to check on Sadie? He did allow the boy and girl to go in first; that would only be right. Especially the girl—she understood the other worlds better than the boy. Maybe he would see that strange cat again, if it was a cat.

Ida Belle did perceive the situation very well, except why could she not know for sure if it was Joseph who was responsible for the visions and maybe other things as well? Oh well, *she thought,* I will find out if it is Joseph; who else can it be?

The second cavern was not as old as the first, and the drawings were not as worn; nevertheless there was no sign of Whitedeer or the clan's sacred objects. Jack was first to leave the cavern, catching a glimpse of the elusive cat coming out of the last cavern. He would not let a cat get the best of him; still, maybe it was not just a cat.

Joseph and Ida Belle followed Jack into the third cavern; it was much newer than the first two, with stone benches and shelves carved into the walls. Joseph had noticed the light was getting dimmer and suggested that they hurry. In the shelves they found two pipes and the remains of the clan's sacred bundles. Ida Belle at first was very happy, then realized they had fulfilled only half their promise.

Joseph agreed but believed if there were more signs to what happened to Whitedeer they would have to come back when it would be lighter in the cavern. Ida Belle agreed but was reluctant to leave and decided to stay a little while longer. Once again she felt a presence in some way guiding her toward a dimly lit corner of the cavern. What is this? Isa Belle thought as she noticed a stick with unusual figures carved on it.

Chapter Twenty-seven:

Thinking in the Way
of the Ancestors

Sadie could sense the tension Joseph was feeling as they followed Jack and the goat herd back to the pens. She could not know what the matter was but tried not to bother him. It had become the boy's custom to run beside her instead of riding on her back when he needed to solve some problem, but this was different; she had not seen him like this before.

This time she would stay behind the boy just to make sure he would be all right. It was not only that for some things she needed him; it was because he never mistreated her or made her do the stupid things other horses had to do. Best of all he shared all his fodder with her—and, well, with the dog too. For a moment she considered why she tolerated that dog. Most dogs were just a nuisance and always in the way.

Joseph took his time with his chores when he returned to the stables. There were many things he had neglected before that seemed urgent now. He would work on his totem; there would be four sides; one for each direction.

191

He had not decided how many figures on each side. After a while he could no longer avoid going to the house for the evening meal.

It was as Joseph expected at the supper table that evening; after his performance that day the serious nature of their silence could not be mistaken. He did not mind; he understood—how could they think anything different? If he wanted it to be different it was up to him to conduct his life in a way that allowed them to think of him in a better way. He had to hold back a smile as he thought of how it was that way with Jack and himself.

Ida Belle had quickly finished her kitchen duties and was in Warmwind's room when Joseph finished his meal and came up to be with them. She had wakened her great-grandmother as she came in and was waiting for Joseph before telling her of the caverns and finding the clan's sacred objects.

Warmwind could see Ida Belle was anxious to tell her of their day, but not Joseph; it was just as well, for she must tell them it was time for her to end the visit and return to her home on the reservation. Maybe she should tell them now. Warmwind said, "Before you tell me of your adventures today I must tell you in less than a week I will be returning home to the reservation."

Joseph had not thought about his great-grandmother leaving. Then he considered his sister. He knew how much she enjoyed her company and how they talked a lot, mostly about woman stuff. He would miss her, but maybe she would be more comfortable around her things, and she must have friends there.

Ida Belle had enjoyed her great-grandmother's company; except for her brother she felt closer to her than anyone else. In a way she was disappointed in that Warmwind had given up her role as a seer or gifted one, but she knew it was not for her to question destiny or the great unknown one. The thought of telling her great-grandmother about finding the secluded caverns gave her a sense of sorrow, and she did not know why.

Joseph was first to speak of the caverns. "Great-grandmother, we have found three caverns hidden within one of the rock formations. The remains of the sacred bundles were there along with other things but not a sign of Whitedeer.

"There were many symbols and drawings on the walls of the caverns; some of the drawings must have been there for many years. It must have been as you have said, instead of writing in books the pictures tell much more."

Warmwind thanked the twins and told them they had done well; would they tell her more about the caverns? Ida Belle explained about the village scene and of the dream, waiting for her great-grandmother to tell her it was so.

After a few moments of silence, Warmwind began to utter her thoughts out loud. "It was around the time of Whitedeer's disappearance that some religious leaders were reluctant to perform the rituals and dances that taught the sacred knowledge of the ancient priest, the men of mystery.

"Yes, and it was also the time many in our tribe turned away from the old ways; they turned to new religions and refused to even speak of earlier times." Warmwind paused and then with unmistakable frustration put forward the question of "Why until now?"

Ida Belle asked her great-grandmother if she was all right. Warmwind only responded by telling the twins they must return to the caverns but this time not to think in the way of their generation but let their thoughts wander, searching with their minds.

Ida Belle, after acknowledging her great-grandmother, excused herself to leave, motioning to Joseph to do the same. Joseph accepted his sister's judgment, remembering the mystical charm and overpowering magnetism he had felt about her at the caverns.

In some way, he realized, he had always considered his sister as somewhat out of the ordinary, but always it was just as his little sister. He began to think about why. The spell, if that what it was, made him realize his *knowledge of his sister was only a small part of her, opening his mind to question what else around him he was not conscious of.*

The next day Joseph had arranged to meet Ida Belle at the entrance to the three caverns after he finished helping Rubin with preparations for the upcoming cutting horse competition. Warmwind had warned them about telling anyone what they had discovered.

Joseph was getting used to working with Alvin's horse, although he sometimes wished it would not wait for his every command before making a move. She was a good horse and very fast, but without Alvin's ability to anticipate the every move of the cows Joseph could only hope he would not have to compete in the horse cutting event.

At last Rubin was satisfied with the performance of his horse and decided he was as ready as he would ever be. Alvin agreed, but asked Joseph to work the cows once more, saying, "This time, do not wait for the cow to make her move but think what you would do if you were the cow; then direct Ellie to move into position to respond to it."

Joseph at first found it difficult to think what a cow would do then with a little practice began to get better. Even though his brothers were pleased with his performance, Joseph knew it was not good enough. That was okay, though; a cattle man he would never be, just as his brothers would never be the warrior he was.

When Joseph had separated the cow herd into their respective weight groups without any fault, the cows were herded back to pastures and Joseph hurried off to meet Ida Belle at the caverns. It was good to be riding Sadie; she seemed to know from his thoughts just what to do—well, maybe his movements.

Ida Belle had returned to the caverns ahead of time; she wanted to look at the stick she had found the day before. Warmwind had suddenly become serious and starting murmuring things that had no meaning right after hearing about the stick. In the night it had become apparent to Ida Belle that the stick in some way had something to do with the tribe turning away from their ancestral ways.

Well, *Ida Belle thought as she brought the stick out of the cavern and examined it more closely,* in a way it is special, but why did Great-grandmother attach so much importance to it? *Joseph had come up behind his sister and was pleased that he had accomplished something without her knowing it first.*

Ida Belle, seeing Joseph's delight, hurled the stick at him. Joseph caught the stick, only to feel energy within the stick pulling him toward a painting on the wall.

In disbelief he handed the stick back to Ida Belle who then continued to speak of the ancestors. It was not a spell like he had originally thought. Ida Belle returned the stick back to where she had found it. Neither Ida Belle nor Joseph could talk of it.

Joseph was first to shake off the experience as just more of the same weird stuff and say it's time they started looking for signs that told them about what happened to Whitedeer. Ida Belle could only nod her agreement and begin to search with her brother.

After a while Joseph asked, "Do you suppose that the stick and the drawings are about the same things?"

Ida Belle answered, "Yes, it is just as you say; we do not have to search for signs of Whitedeer any longer." *Ida Belle could feel her whole existence become one with Whitedeer and with the struggle she had endured to protect and preserve an unbroken lineage. Now it would become her destiny, her fate, to carry on the thoughts and rituals of her ancestors.*

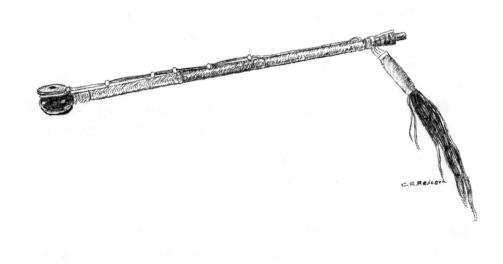

Chapter Twenty-eight:

The prayer stick

"Great-grandmother," Ida Belle said, not waiting for the normal formalities, "I know Joseph is not the one of which we spoke of. I must know."

Warmwind was silent for what seemed like forever to Ida Belle before speaking. "There are some things that are not spoken of but reside in the minds of those who experience the thoughts that are sacred and mysterious. It is not for me to say."

Ida Belle could not avoid the reality that within her family another had been present guiding her, teaching her in the shadowiness of both the middle waters and the other worlds of nature and spirit. It was strange that Great-grandmother obviously did not know who it was either. She searched her mind for who it could be, but it was though a giant wall prevented her from entering.

Her thoughts became more focused as she heard Joseph coming up the stairs; the one who was gifted and more clever than she would not be obvious or perceptible. There were two in the family she had disregarded by virtue of their humble, unassuming nature.

Joseph asked Great-grandmother to excuse him this night, because tomorrow he would have to be at the cattle corral early. Before he left he asked her about the finely carved stick. It must have been of some importance because it was left in the caverns.

Warmwind answered, "I can only tell you in the time of my grandfather there was talk of such carved objects called prayer sticks used by the holy men to perform rituals; some said they were passed down from the men of mystery and possess inner meaning and powers hidden from those unworthy within the carvings."

Ida Belle called to Joseph as he left the room, "You must not think of things always in a physical way."

Joseph was up early the next morning; he could not forget what his sister had said last night about always thinking in a physical way. He had learned that even though his sister said odd things, she always seemed to know something was going to happen. It would be the last day to prepare for the cutting horse contest, and he could not shake an uneasy feeling that something might happen to Rubin.

Both Jack and Sadie were waiting for Joseph when he arrived at the stables. Their universe was the boy, and when he was not at ease within himself their lives were troubled. "That's it!" Joseph roared. "You too!" Instead of scouting ahead of the goat herd, the Great Pyrenees were quietly walking by his side with an occasional glance to see what was the matter.

Jack found a suitable site to pasture the goat herd and with an appreciative gesture signaled the Great Pyrenees to take over the watch. Sadie had followed the boy and Great Pyrenees all the way from the coral; on the way back she nudged him until he reluctantly gave in to her demands and climbed on her back. Joseph almost forgot his problem as he rode Sadie, galloping through the fields with Jack along side.

When Joseph arrived at the cattle pens it was not difficult to see Rubin was preoccupied during his first exercise with cutting out the smaller cows.

Alvin had left the arena and was just sitting on the bleachers, not wanting to think about what was happening. Rubin, seeing Joseph and Alvin sitting together, reined in his horse and came over to them.

Joseph was the first to speak. "What is the matter?"

Alvin replied, "It is the war; most of the Wazhazhe men of age have already joined the army."

Rubin explained that today was the day the army would send his orders; the orders would say whether he'd passed the medical physical and, if he did, when he must leave. They all agreed that Joseph would exercise both horses and continue working the cattle.

It was difficult for Joseph to keep his concentration on working the cattle. Neither horse responded very well to his movements, although Alvin's horse was faster and could move better. It was agreed that if he had to ride in the contest, it would be with Alvin's horse. Joseph tried to do his best but was glad when it was time to return the cows to pasture and bring in the goat herd.

Ida Belle was waiting for Joseph at the stables with the news that Rubin would have to leave the next day. Joseph and Alvin would be leaving for the fairgrounds early the next morning. Joseph had to ask about what the family was saying. Ida Bell could only respond that most were quiet and were disappointed, believing he was not experienced and knew very little about working cattle.

Joseph thanked her and quietly went about finishing up his chores; if he was to leave the next morning there was the goat herd to consider as well as Sadie and Jack. He would bring the horse Alvin rode but leave Rubin's horse; Sadie would take her place behind the buckboard to keep her company. With extra hay the goat herd would be all right in the new, fenced pasture.

Nothing was mentioned at the evening meal about the cutting horse competition. The conversation centered mostly on Rubin and the army.

Joseph was not sure if it was because everyone was being polite or they just considered it no longer possible to win the prize money.

Joseph at first considered not going to his great-grandmother's room. It was the last chance he would have to talk with her before she left for the reservation. He would ask her about the rituals and legends.

Warmwind was most pleased with her visit and happy to talk to the twins once more before going back to the reservation, the dilemma that had bothered her for so long now resolved. In a strange way she could see the same conflict in the twins, especially Joseph.

She could once more hear Joseph and Ida Belle coming up the stairs without talking. There was silence in the room until Joseph asked his great-grandmother how could he believe the impossible legends and what were the traditions all about? Warmwind smiled and answered him by saying they were both ways of explaining the inner meaning of that which was symbolic in nature.

Ida Belle had sat down quietly and did not want to interfere but had to ask about the drawings and the contents within the caverns. What were they all about and what was a prayer stick? Warmwind replied that she was not the one they should be asking, but she would tell them all she knew.

"Our forefathers used symbols to communicate ideas, our history, and sayings of the men of mystery. The drawings may be replicas of the tribal rituals that through symbolism tell of early Wazhazhe life and of sacred knowledge handed down from the men of mystery. You must remember there is some truth in myths and legends.

"If in the caverns the drawings do not convey meaning and purpose to you, they are probably not of the tribal rituals."

Both Ida Belle and Joseph could not keep from thinking about the village scene at the entrance of the first cavern and how they were drawn to it.

"About the prayer stick," Warmwind continued, "it may have been sort of a tally stick that the priest used to keep track of their place in the rituals. If you think of the rituals as being in the form of songs, then each single carving on the prayer stick would represent a song. I have heard that the songs were sometimes misleading just to keep the sacred knowledge safe from those not adequate."

Joseph, believing that his great-grandmother and sister were just talking a lot of nonsense, excused himself because he was to leave early the next morning for the fair and the cutting horse contest. Ida Belle too excused herself; she would begin making plans to visit the caverns and begin deciphering the drawings.

Ida Belle allowed what her great-grandmother had said to become focused in her mind: Then if the drawings in the caverns are rituals, each picture symbolizes a song, and some parts of the song may be misleading; the tally, or prayer stick, is the key to deciphering the ritual's inner purpose or meaning—an invitation to follow.

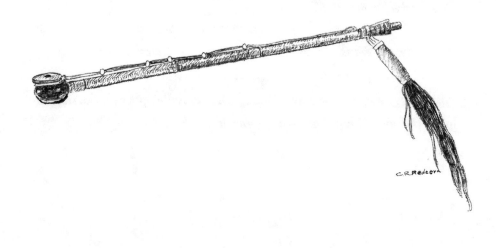

CHAPTER TWENTY-NINE:

A SENSE OF UNIQUENESS

It was a solemn occasion the next morning as the family said goodbye to Rubin on his way to join an army unit with friends and relatives from the Wazhazhe reservation. It was also a fulfillment of many generations as Rubin represented the clan in this war; a member of the family and clan had served in every war in which their nation was ever involved.

Alvin and Joseph had set out earlier that morning to compete in the cutting horse competition. They would spend one night on the trail before reaching their destination. The team of horses pulling the buckboard with two horses tied behind drew little attention. Joseph could only wish it were himself instead of Rubin going to war.

By late morning the team had reached the Oklahoma territory; Alvin and Joseph watched the sky begin to turn dark, showing signs of a storm brewing ahead. Alvin and Joseph had not considered they would run into a storm; they would soon turn south into Texas right into the storm. There was not enough time to reach the fair grounds, and they would have to find shelter losing valuable time.

The storm caused them to arrive at the fairgrounds four hours later than planned; what was worse, Alvin's horse, Nellie, had become ill from the heavy, wet rain. They had only two hours to revive Nille and prepare for Josephs ride. Ida Belle had made up a pack containing all the provisions they would need; the herbs to give Nille was included.

It was no use; Nille was gradually recovering but would not be able to work the cattle in the wet muddy arena. Alvin left it up to Joseph to either cancel or to ride Sadie. So many things flashed through Joseph's consciousness; would Sadie be okay with the large crowd, what about a saddle and she had never worked with cattle?

Joseph remembered how Sadie had handled the goats; they were more difficult than the cattle and he had stayed on with his homemade saddle blanket. It had puzzled him how she had responded to his movements as commands. It was settled he would ride Sadie with his Indian saddle and the single rawhide rope loosely around her lower jaw.

When it was Joseph turn to work his allotment of cattle the officials could not agree if his gear was authorized and too dangerous. They each had to examine his home made saddle and the raw hide strap that fit easily around Sadie's lower jaw; It was decided that it was risky but so was everything else about the rodeo; seeing the response from the audience they had to agree. Finally the cattle were brought into the arena.

What Joseph had not thought of was how he would get back on Sadie in front of the crowd. Joseph let his mind search for an answer. Almost instantly the memory of the eagle cries and the flapping of her wings filled his mind and he flew onto Sadie's back.

Instantly Sadie had leaped into action responding to Joseph reassuring touch;

Like in a dream Joseph could sense his mind open up to a greater awareness, a multidimensional insight without his conscious reasoning. Somewhere in his subconscious a chant begin to emerge.

Is it not unlike an eagle, as I soar
rising above the boundaries of my mind,
conscious of that which is observed from beyond?
Is it not unlike an eagle, as I ride,
soaring within the wind that is my balance,
alert to the turbulence of that which occurs beneath?

> *Is it not unlike an eagle, as I pursue,*
> *searching the sky and lands to fulfill my destiny,*
> *always being watchful without being confident?*

When the last cow was sorted out Sadie circled the arena before passing through the finishing line and back to the stables. It was not important to Joseph that they had won. His horse was wet and covered with mud. He would wash her off and rub her down; was it not what was expected of him?

As he watched, in some way Jack understood the bond and confidence that had taken place between the boy and horse—not that it was okay for a cattle dog like himself, but for a horse and a human it was okay. If he could just get the smell of all the cooking sorted out—he would have to investigate.

Jack found that he could obtain the good smelling stuff from almost every place they cooked it if he conducted himself in the right way. He knew Joseph would be all right with Sadie, and the opportunity did not come that often. He did wonder about the thing the man Alvin had brought back to the buckboard.

The judges had reached a decision and announced Joseph as the winner. Alvin and Joseph along with Sadie returned to the arena to accept the prize money and to have their pictures taken. Joseph after much persuasion brought out his homemade blanket saddle and replaced Sadie's halter with the rawhide strap.

When all the ceremonies ended and the horses were taken care of, Alvin and Joseph toured the fairgrounds. Joseph was interested in the horses, and Alvin was especially interested in the cattle judging events. It was very good, but everyone seemed to be paying attention to them. It became clear when one man asked if they would sell Sadie.

"Maybe we should leave," Alvin reluctantly acknowledged. Back at the campgrounds Joseph turned his attention to Jack; it was obvious the dog was not feeling well, although it was not as it was with Alvin's horse so maybe it was something more serious. Had something happened while he was busy with the contest?

Alvin assured him not to worry—Jack had eaten so much from the fairgrounds he probably would be sick for days. It was late into the night when the last person had stopped by to congratulate them and to see the horse that caused all the excitement.

Joseph could see Sadie was enjoying every minute of it. It occurred to him what his third totem would be; this time he would know if it was his sister influencing his totem.

Sarah lost her concentration on the journal. She could not help thinking, what was it that her great-grandfather had experienced that was so important to him? The obvious was that he had experienced thoughts allowing his mind to go into a state where he became conscious of things through their appearance.

She was sure he was not the one who wrote the journal. It could not have been Alvin or Rubin. No, it had to be someone else who wrote the journal and that person must have been in every way perceptive of that which was written in the journal.

It would have to be someone that endured in the shadows, responsible for influencing the destinies of those encountered, someone with the powers and sensitive of the invisible world—someone like Hanna or Quinton.

Maybe it was true of all those who came after, the children of the middle water. But then there was no reason to believe it had to be a girl or there was only one.

Sarah could not help wondering how this could be happening to her. She had visited the same caverns written about in the journal, and, yes, there was an influence or magnetism from within the drawings to her as well, just as Ida Belle had experienced in the journal.

How could this be possible? If it was possible then what else was probable, even promising? She returned to the cavern entrance, where she could see the old, faded drawings and brought out the journal.

Sarah become aware that Hanna was calling her from the entrance of the caverns. Suddenly she was there by her side, and in some way must have known what she had just read. "Hanna," Sarah softly whispered, "is this journal in some way an invitation for us to follow?"

There was no need for an answer.

Chapter Thirty:

Book of poems

"You must come quickly," Hanna warned her; in the distance Sarah could see her grandfather and some of her cousins approaching the river. Thinking they must be looking for her, she tucked the journal into the saddlebags and rode down the other side of the river where she could cross ahead of them.

It would be easy to explain she had ridden a good distance without thinking about the time. The cousins were first to greet her with news of newfound artifacts discovered in the cave. They had found another old journal that looked like a book of poems. Sarah was at first baffled when her grandfather gave her the book.

This journal was smaller than the others, and in the journal she found the three poems were the chants, as Joseph would call them, she had read in the first journal. The rest of the poems she had not read before. Sarah took her time after reaching the stables to determine what she should do.

Misty looked on with interest but gave no response when the girl looked to her for an answer. Still, Misty could sense her companion was distressed and would like to have helped. Sarah was not sure if she should explain that the first three poems were in the first journal too.

That would mean she would have to explain about Joseph and Ida Belle also. No! It was clear she was not to reveal the contents of the first journal. Finally she had to return to the ranch house.

Sarah was relieved the conversation around the evening meal was about the ceremonial room. It was an exciting time for the family, as some would organize different events. One cousin asked if she would like to participate in one of the dances. Sarah said no, she was very happy spending time with Hanna and Misty as they explored the ranch.

Just as everyone had finished with the evening meal, Sarah's uncle John asked her if she had seen the journal found in the cave. Trying to end the exchange, she responded, "Yes, but I have not heard what you will be doing at the ceremonies."

It was no use—the subject of the journal had come up, and it became the main topic of discussion. Ultimately James was asked to read the first poem.

He consented only after encouraging glances from both Sarah and Hanna urged him to continue. As her grandfather began to read the poem Sarah remembered him telling her that the storytellers had become the artist and teachers.

What has brought me to this valley,
a cry in the night?
The cougar led the way
to bring me to this native land.
She drinks from the stream without fear;
why does she not realize the hunter that I am?
Who has brought me to this valley,
a cry in the night?

> The cougar led the way
> to awaken me to this native land.
> She is not what she seems;
> an apparition or prophecy she must be.
> Who has brought me to this valley,
> spirits in the night?
> The cougar led the way
> to consider this native land.
> Why have I been chosen?
> A believer in spirits I am not.

When he had finished there was silence in the room until one of her younger cousins said, "Sarah must know of such things; tell us what it means." At that the rest of the room echoed the appeal for her to explain what it was all about.

With thanks she said, "You give me too much credit. I can only try.

"The poem is of a young warrior," Sarah began, "pleased with his life and the world around him. While hunting a cougar, he ventures into a valley unlike any he has ever known before. It is unfamiliar to him, revealing a part of himself he does not understand. He cannot relate what he is experiencing with the realities that he knows to be true.

"He searches for the identity of what or who has awakened him to such consciousness. The young warrior questions the existence of powers beyond his understanding and then rejects the supernatural world of spirits."

There were requests, even demands, for the poem to be read again, and there was absolute agreement with her interpretation of the poem. With a great deal of encouragement, James was persuaded to read another poem. He knew which poem Sarah wanted him to read next.

Do not suffer the weakness of fright;
spirits make fun of our fear in the night.
Let them send the thunder likened to buffalos
racing through the heavens.
Let them send the winds likened to dark spirits
twisting and howling.
Do not suffer the weakness of fright;
spirits make fun of our fear in the night.
Is it not the ancestors that look to see bravery
at the time of our trial?
Is it not the ancestors that record our courage
at the time of our peril?

This time he was asked to read the poem over again and then once more. Everyone had their version of what the poem was about. Unable to decide who was right, they asked their cousin Sarah once again to tell them what the poem was about.

"It is of a time when the warrior in the first poem and a companion must undergo great danger. He chants his poem to keep up his courage and that of his companion. He is unable to avoid the ravaging of a great storm; it is the mischievous spirits racing through the sky that has brought the lightening, wind, and rain.

"To keep up his courage he speaks to the ancestors that surely must be watching; appealing to them to record into the history of the Wazhazhe nation his bravery and courage. The poem does not tell us much about his companion, except his friend had lost courage, and the young warrior was comforting him."

It was agreed that Sarah's interpretation was the best, although there was some uncertainty about the companion, if there was one.

James could see that everyone was waiting for him to read the next poem. "I will read one more," he responded as he began to read once more, this time the one that interested him most.

Is it not unlike an eagle, as I soar,
rising above the boundaries of my mind,
conscious of that which is observed from beyond?
Is it not unlike an eagle, as I ride,
soaring within the wind that is my balance,
alert to the turbulence of that which occurs beneath?
Is it not unlike an eagle, as I pursue,
searching the sky and lands to fulfill my destiny,
always being watchful without being confident?

When James had finished, all eyes were on Sarah. Sarah at first agreed but then had second thoughts, saying, "I would, but there is someone who could explain it better than I." The family all agreed that they wanted to hear an explanation of the poem from such a person. Sarah then said, "That would be Hanna."

Hanna realized that Sarah was uncomfortable with the poem, so she agreed to interpret it, saying, "I will explain the poem as best I can; but, please, you must tell me what you would like to know."

One cousin was quick to say, "The poem is about an eagle, not a warrior isn't it? How could a warrior soar like an eagle?"

"Not exactly—the one writing the poem is writing about how the young warrior uses the imagery of an eagle to describe what he is experiencing. He does not soar like an eagle; he lets his mind soar in a way that is like an eagle soaring. Let me read it to you once more.

> *"Is it not unlike an eagle, as I soar;*
> *rising above the borders of my mind;*
> *conscious of that which is observed from beyond?"*

"Okay, that may be," said another cousin. "What about the next part where he says, 'as I ride'?"

"Let me read that part over again for you," Hanna answered. "This time, imagine what he could be riding that he experience the flight of an eagle.

> *"Is it not unlike an eagle, as I ride;*
> *soaring within the wind that is my balance;*
> *alert to the turbulence of that which occurs beneath?"*

There was complete silence in the room until one cousin spoke, saying ,"He could be riding in a rodeo... maybe a bucking horse or Brahma bull."

"Very good. Now I will read the last part," Hanna quietly replied.

> *"It is not unlike an eagle, as I pursue;*
> *searching the sky and lands to fulfill my destiny;*
> *always being watchful without being confident?"*

When there was no one willing to speak, Hanna asked, "Have you ever noticed an eagle will build as many as six nests at one time—always on the move as if it was searching for what is necessary or inevitable to fulfill its destiny?"

For a moment the room became quiet, and Hanna thought she had explained the poem to everyone's satisfaction. Then many spoke at once asking who the young warrior was.

Hanna answered, "Yes, it is a mystery when the book was written and who it was that put the poems in writing." However, she believed the poem could have been written for Sarah's benefit.

Sarah's grandfather thanked her and changed the subject, fully aware Hanna knew the young warrior was his father. His father had always been one of mystery and intrigue, always centered and balanced in the midst of disorder.

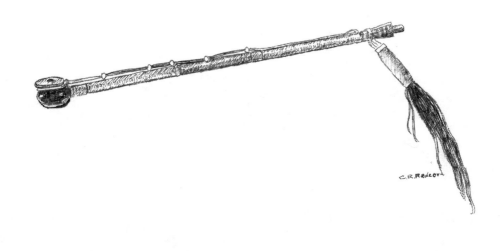

Part Seven:

SURVIVAL IN THE VISIBLE WORLD: "SYMBOLISM"

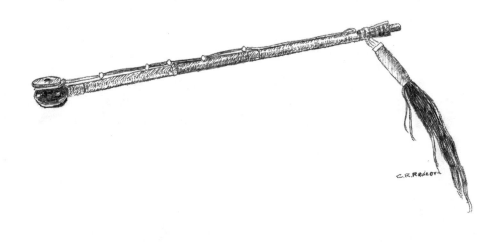

Chapter Thirty-one:

Images and inner meaning

It was early the next morning when Alvin and Joseph harnessed up the team, beginning their trip back to the ranch. This time Jack rode in the buckboard huddled up as close as he could to Joseph. Alvin drove the team, taking care; Nellie's condition had improved, but they would have to travel slowly, allowing her to rest.

Along about mid-morning Alvin stopped at a place near a stream, allowing the horses to drink and rest for a while. It was not long before a crowd had gathered. A man gave them a newspaper telling about the cutting horse event; there were pictures of Sadie showing the homemade saddle. Sadie had become a famous celebrity overnight.

It was a strange and wonderful time for Alvin and Joseph. They were not use to being noticed, but they did enjoy all the food that they were given. Joseph could not help seeing a girl about Alvin's age slip him a piece of paper that he quickly read and tucked safely away. Alvin then suspiciously examined Nellie and pronounced, "We will have to camp here tonight."

Joseph could not agree more—he wanted to sort out his thoughts, and Jack was not feeling very good as well. Alvin drove the team to a grove of trees not far from a small general store. Joseph wondered how he knew of *the store but disregarded it as just luck—that was until the same girl that gave Alvin the note came out of the store.*

It was not of importance; Joseph heated some of the same herbs that Ida Belle had given to Jack once before. Jack remembered the smell and how they had made him feel better; there was also a sufficient amount for Nellie. Sadie watched with interest as Joseph first gave Nellie some of the herb medicine from his hand and then held the pan of medicine for her to drink.

Joseph first noticed a small boy peeking from behind the buckboard. That in itself was not of interest to Joseph, but it started him to thinking; it was the way the boy wanted to look but not be seen.

Before yesterday he would not have given it a second thought, but today he realized it was possibly how Ida Belle knew so much. If in everything there is an inner meaning or purpose that can be made known through its imagery, then that is how Jack and Sadie act in response to my imagery.

Joseph could not wait to confront both of them, although they were both more experienced and who knew what else they made use of. No, he would have to be very secretive about it.

Joseph began to consider all the possibilities: first even though he was not aware of it he was using imagery to communicate ideas and information with Jack and Sadie. Second, what about there being different levels of meaning? He could easily mistake the meaning or purpose of an image. Third, there could be many images that have multiple meanings. This was more difficult than he first thought.

For a moment Joseph could not decide what to do next. It was Sadie that first gave out a neigh, then Jack put both his paws on Joseph's lap. Okay, Joseph thought. He could not keep any secrets from them; they would be his teachers. He must look a mess to them.

Joseph's next thoughts were of Ida Belle. How could he conceal from her what he had experienced or of his new awareness? No, that would be impossible, but he could maybe give the wrong impression. Maybe let her think he got the wrong meaning or purpose; at least until he had gained enough experience, then it would be all right to tell her.

His thoughts turned to the totem pole. Would he be able to finish the third totem without her influence, or at least know where it was coming from? Something or someone was helping him.

Joseph then turned his attention to the general store; it was obviously run by an Indian family, maybe Quapaw. He was sure they were not Wazhazhe but must be closely related. Living on the ranch, his family had given up most of their social and religious traditions; this family or families had not.

There was smoke coming from the chimney with the window shutters opened. That would mean it was not for heating; someone was either cooking food or using the fire to craft something. Joseph shook his head, thinking, No that was just using normal logic and reasoning ,not anything special.

Then the girl he had seen earlier came out of the store wearing a traditional Indian dress carrying a box of food. Joseph could not remember if she was wearing the dress before. She was of the Quapaw tribe, and he did not know that from normal logic and reasoning. It was through the imagery or symbolism that he had learned that they were of a traditional Indian family.

When Alvin followed her out of the store Joseph could not believe the way he acted. Joseph first wondered if he had drunk something that made him so empty-headed, then thought maybe he had fallen and hit his head. Whatever it was, it scared Joseph more than the eagle had or maybe even more than the silence after hearing a rattlesnake.

The girl, Susette, prepared a place for them to eat, and Joseph could see clearly that Alvin had lost all his common sense. He is like a little boy around that girl, *Joseph thought; maybe Ida Belle had packed a herb that would straighten him out.*

Alvin did become serious while they were eating and suggested that he should stay for a while to make sure Nellie was well enough to travel. Tomorrow Joseph would return alone, letting everyone know he was all right and would come later.

The rest of the evening Alvin brought Joseph up to date on all that was needed to work the cattle, at least for the next two weeks. It would best if the buckboard stayed with him. Joseph could not help thinking his brother was not coming back to work the ranch. It was true his injuries would keep him from most all of the ranch activities, but he was still needed.

Everyone was up early the next morning; to Joseph's surprise Susette had been up earlier and had prepared breakfast and a lunch sack for him too. Joseph, seeing Alvin and Susette together, could not ignore how much they reminded him of his first memories of his father and mother. Alvin handed Joseph a letter addressed to their father and wished him a safe journey.

Jack was eager to lead off, as if to say, I know the way back to the ranch—follow me. *After a short while Joseph relaxed and allowed Jack and Sadie to travel at their own pace. It was strange that he had never noticed how Jack and Sadie interacted with each other before, especially if he did not get involved.*

His mind began to wander, thinking only three months ago he was not allowed to go into the rugged mountains. Now he had ridden in the cutting horse competition and was traveling by himself. He had his two companions to thank for all that had taken place since then. What of Ida Belle? Yes, she had always known the ways he was feeling now.

It was late in the evening when Joseph reached the stables. He fed and brushed Sadie, making sure Jack had his dog food and he was settled in for the night. He could not shake the strange feeling even though everything was the same it seemed not to be the same. It must be he had changed and he just looked at things differently. Must be the thing about images have inner meaning and different levels of meanings.

Ida Belle had seen the light reflecting from Joseph's lantern as he attended to Jack and Sadie. She was reluctant to go out to meet him but knew there was something unusual, out of the ordinary, and had to investigate. They were twins, and even though they were sister and brother there was a supernatural bond between them she could feel growing.

Joseph, hearing the soft footsteps of his sister coming into the stables, was determined this time not to let his sister know everything he had experienced or become aware of, if that was possible. It then came to him that if he could control the image— that symbolic stuff—he was giving off, he could control what his sister perceived of him.

Ida Belle called out to be certain it was Joseph that came into the stables; with so much happening she had reservations about what she actually perceived. With the sound of Joseph's voice telling her he was here getting his saddlebag, her confidence reemerged with a greater determination than ever.

As they walked to the ranch house together, each one was aware it would not be as it was before, each one searching for a sense of balance in the midst of their escalating world. What they knew for certain was that they had relied on one another in the past and always would in the future even more now that Great-grandmother was not with them.

Everyone had gathered in the kitchen and was waiting for Joseph to tell them the news. Joseph noticed the newspaper showing Sadie's picture on the kitchen table. Its imagery conveyed to him he did not have to tell them about the contest, only about Alvin. Joseph removed Alvin's letter from his saddlebag and handed it to his father.

Joseph explained about encountering the storm and how Nellie had become ill, how Alvin stayed behind to make sure she would be able to make the return trip, but he did not tell them about Susette until his father inquired why would it take two weeks, and did Joseph know why Alvin borrowed the money they had won in the contest?

Ida Belle could see Joseph was embarrassed and not sure what he should say. She asked where Alvin was staying and who he was with.

Joseph, knowing he would never think of deceiving his sister again, began to tell about meeting Susette and of the general store. Afterwards he did not mind as Ida Belle watched him complete the third totem of Sadie as he competed in the cutting horse competition.

CHAPTER THIRTY-TWO:

THE INVISIBLE WORLD

The morning came early for Joseph. He could hear his father moving around in the kitchen; with Rubin in the military and Alvin still not recovered from his injury it was up to him to help his father. It did feel good to be needed even though he still did not want to spend his life working with cattle or goats.

This morning his mother brought Joseph coffee, and his father congratulated him on winning the contest. His father continued, saying that there had been many offers to buy Sadie but she was his horse to do with what he wanted. Joseph did not have to be told that until Alvin recovered and Rubin returned, much would be expected of him.

Together they discussed a new strategy to manage both the cattle and goats. Joseph was glad his brother had taken the time to explain what was needed and how he should go about it. With each word Joseph spoke he could see his father in some way must have known what he was going to say before he said it. It did make sense—his father and mother would know about symbolism and images.

To Joseph's delight Ida Belle came out of the kitchen just to refill his coffee cup. She knew that their discovery of the caverns would have to wait *until Joseph sorted out his new responsibilities. That did not mean she could not slip off to the caverns to discover as much as she could for both of them. She was sure the prayer stick was the means to unravel the mystery of the drawings.*

Joseph found both Jack and Sadie waiting for him in the pasture behind the stables. In some mysterious way he could tell there had been some sort of disagreement. Sadie, she would want to run and jump through the pasture while Jack wanted to get back to work. Well, now, *Joseph thought,* I know just what will satisfy both of you.

It was time to cut out the older calves from the herd before turning the bulls into the herd. Alvin had told Joseph how to bring the herd into the largest pen, where he could cut out the calves, herding them into another pen that opened to a smaller, secure pasture. The trick would be to keep them separated as he cut the next calf out of the herd.

Neither Jack nor Sadie was too happy when Joseph opened the gate to move the goats out of their pasture and into the open hillside, but they responded to his needs. They even went along with him when he did not stop to explore an area of the ranch where they had never been.

It was when they came upon the cattle herd that they became once again companions, a team. It did not take Jack long to bring the herd into order.

With Joseph and Sadie leading the way, Jack followed, moving the herd behind them. Joseph was sure Jack looked at least six inches taller than normal. It did not take Jack long to drive the cattle into the largest pen when Joseph opened the gate.

Joseph was not sure what to do next but decided to cut one calf out of the herd and move it into the calves' pen. Sadie seemed to know what was asked of her and waited only to know which calf was first. Jack remembered the time before when they were practicing for the cutting horse competition and waited by the open gate.

When Joseph selected a larger calf Sadie went into action, cutting out the calf and moving it into the open pen. Joseph had only to pick out a heifer; Sadie would cut it out of the herd and move it into the calves' pen. Jack stood guard over the gate, not allowing the calves to come out or the cows to go in.

When all the larger calves were cut out of the herd and securely locked in their pen, Joseph and Sadie followed as Jack drove the cows back to open pasture. It was time to explore the valley and search for the best fruits and grasses. When they came upon some blackberries that were just right for eating, Joseph and Jack quickly found the best way to pick the berries without being stuck.

Sadie tried but soon gave up, giving out a shrill neigh. Joseph at first laughed, then after picking a couple of brier thorns from Sadie's muzzle, started picking a handful for her then a handful for himself. When all had eaten what they could, it was time to go back to the livestock pens. This time Jack rode behind Joseph.

When they returned, Joseph's father was there to tell Joseph, "Good job—it normally takes two days to separate the larger calves from the herd." He removed Alvin's letter from his pocket and read once more the part about not needing him since Joseph and his horse Sadie would be there to take care of things for him.

It saddened him to think back to a time long ago when he was his son's age. How history repeats itself—had not his father been in the same circumstance he was now in? He knew Joseph's passion was not in the ranch; well, maybe for the animals. It did not matter how good his son was working the ranch; he would never completely belong to the ranch.

This he knew, for it was that way for himself. He had almost forgotten the prints he had drawn of Indian war parties and of the great buffalo hunts. He had listened to the elders talk of the great buffalo herds, their hunts, and defending their ancestral hunting grounds. Later he would

227

search his mind for the images that had come to him, putting them down in sketches and prints.

By supper time the calves were again separated into pens: those to be sent to the market in one, the most promising bull calves in another, and the best heifer calves in another. There was water and feed still to be taken care of then back to the stables to give Sadie a good rub down and double her ration of grain.

Joseph had not forgotten Jack and brought a special plate of food out to him. As Jack ate the food, Sadie was considering what was up with that dog. He did look bigger and held himself much better. It must be the fun we had with the cows. It was fun when you were left to do the job without interference; dog are lucky—they are usually not bothered by meddlesome humans.

Ida Belle missed visiting with their great-grandmother, especially after the evening meal. Tonight the conversation was mostly about Alvin and the girl Susette. There was much speculation; all Joseph would say was that he would be back in a week or two and not to worry.

The next morning Joseph was up early and had eaten his breakfast when his father came to eat. He had not really liked the taste of coffee, but it was a special thing to have coffee. He would have two cups today as he listened to his father tell him there would be cattle buyers coming to see the calves. It would be his responsibility to check the cattle and goat herds in the morning, not to work Sadie or Jack today as they deserved a rest.

This time when Ida Belle poured his coffee she whispered, "Join me at the caverns after lunch. I have something to show you."

Joseph had to laugh and ask if it was another trance. Something in her eyes let Joseph know it was not the right thing to say. Joseph thought it best to acknowledge her and begin his inspection of the cattle herds first.

Alvin had told Joseph what to look for if he was to check the cattle herd. He was not to look at each one individually but to observe the whole herd; if there was a problem, the one with the problem would stand out. There were pens set up to isolate the sick or injured ones. Joseph was sure Alvin would come back, but something told him he would not be working on the ranch any more.

Jack was watching for the boy from his special place overlooking the ranch house and stables. It troubled him that the boy had become very good at predicting his behavior. It had always been to his advantage to foresee what the boy would do or want to do.

Now the boy was beginning to foresee what was about to happen and was learning to avoid some things. Joseph came out of the house and looked up to where Jack was waiting as if to say, Come on, my dog, let's go to work. *It was too much for Jack, who took it as a direct challenge. He knew his job and would do his best on the job, but the rest of the time… well, he just would not put up with it.*

Sadie was also waiting for Joseph; he always brought an apple or carrot, but most of all he was more of a companion than a human. This morning she noticed the dog was a little different. It did not matter—they were on their way where she could run, jump, and find good things to eat.

It did not take long before Jack understood they were looking for the cattle herd. With his keen sense of smell he led the way. It was his job, and he would not hold it over the boy; still it was very reassuring to be in control. Just the same, Jack gave out a commanding bark when he found the cattle herd.

Sadie was a little puzzled at first when the boy wanted to circle the herd. It was all right though, because she began a relaxing trot and could stretch out her legs. Jack was well aware of what the boy was doing; he remembered it was the same as at the ranch he was at before he came to this one.

Joseph was watching for an injured or sick cow when he noticed Jack had stopped and was looking toward one cow; sure enough, the cow was favoring one leg. Sadie had also become aware of the attention that was given to the cow and swung around given Joseph a better look.

Joseph had only to shift his weight to let Sadie know to cut the cow out of the herd. Almost like it had been planned ahead, Joseph and Sadie followed Jack as he brought the cow back to the cattle pens. Joseph made sure the cow had water and feed before returning to the cattle for another look. This time Sadie was ready for the task at hand and trotted around and through the herd; there were no more cows to cut out of the herd.

It was almost midday when Joseph reached the caverns. He wanted to find a better place for Sadie to pass the time while waiting for him. A short distance away he found a meadow with water and shade trees; it suited Sadie just fine.

After finishing her chores Ida Belle packed a lunch for Joseph and found Silver Star in the stables already saddled with a homemade blanket saddle like the one Joseph made for Sadie. It was different in that this one had stirrups made from rope and leather.

Ida Belle was pleased with the new blanket saddle. The saddle she had been using was heavy and hard to cinch up. It did not take her long to realize she could give Silver Star commands by just shifting her weight, by leaning forward, or by leaning backwards.

Joseph was waiting for Ida Belle at the entrance of the caverns when she rode up. Ida Belle could not wait to tell Joseph of her discovery as they led Silver Star to the meadow to be with Sadie." It is something that you must see to know."

Both Ida Belle and Joseph paused for a moment before entering the first cavern; the sensation of being at a place where their ancestors stayed and so much history had taken place overwhelmed them. Ida Belle placed the prayer stick in Joseph's hands and began pointing out drawings that matched up to a group of notches on the prayer stick.

Joseph turned the prayer stick around, seeing that there were three sides, and determined each side must correspond to one of the caverns. One look at Ida Belle convinced him he was thinking right. He then remembered what his great-grandmother had told them about the drawings on the walls being symbolic of songs. What type of songs?

Ida Belle led Joseph to a group of drawings in the last cavern that seemed not to be so complicated. Each one told a story or was symbolic like chants or poems that Joseph had sung; she knew they would interest him. For her the middle cavern was the best; she could feel the songs drawing her into the daily lives of her ancestors.

Joseph and Ida Belle begin to communicate their thoughts and Ideas within an inner meaning of their words. After a while there was little need for words.

Sarah suddenly realized she had reached the last page of the journal. She quickly searched through the remaining pages and found these words written on the back page.

Summer has ended—another era, another age; it is a gift, the mystery of an endless journey.

"Of course," Sarah whispered, letting her mind explore all the possibilities. *The journey is endless; it is an ever-reoccurring episode with each new generation or era discovering their heritage and. fulfilling their destiny.*

The one writing the journal would have grown up in a family that would have benefit from both English and French. It would be a family that still retained the knowledge and traditions of the men of mystery, one like Hanna lived in until her grandmother died.

From outside of the rock formation Sarah could hear someone calling. "Sarah, Sarah, it is I, Hanna, You must come quickly—your grandfather is looking all over for you." Sarah waved to Hanna from the rock ledge above the caverns.

On her way through the passage out of the rock formation Sarah could not stop thinking, *The journal must be written for Hanna, but why did she not read the journal?*

Chapter Thirty-three:

Balance in Chaos: "living in the shadows"

Sarah found her grandfather in the renovated council lodge. "Is this a new painting?" she asked, seeing her grandfather hanging a painting on the display board. "Yes," he answered, "I just finished it this morning. What do you see?"

"It is very good," Sarah replied. "The one in the lead would be Joseph on Sadie, Ida Belle would be next on Silver Star, and the dog in front would be Jack. It is of the endless journey, I think. What did you want to see me about?"

"Your parents have sent a message: you are to return no later than Thursday. We will have to leave in two days."

It was not a surprise to Sarah; she knew that school would soon be starting and there were many things that must be taken care of. It did not even surprise her that she finished the journal in time. What of Hanna? She would be looked after here, but it was obvious this was not her home.

"Grandfather, what will happen to Hanna?" Sarah watched her grandfather's expression change.

"No one really knows—it is up to the courts. John is trying to adopt her, but the one handling her case has a problem with her living on the ranch with there being so many children here now. Maybe it would be a good idea to talk to your mom and dad about it."

Sarah rushed out to tell Hanna, then realized, what if they said no or what if the court said no? She could never remember asking her father or mother for anything so important; there was never any need—they always knew what she needed, and it always seemed to happen. No, what was she thinking? She would not need to tell Hanna.

That night when everyone had gone to bed Sarah woke Hanna, saying, "Would you come downstairs with me? I want to call my parents."

Hanna was not asleep. She had heard that Sarah would be leaving in two days and lay awake unable to sleep. It was not that she was worried about herself; it was for her friend. "Is there anything wrong?" Hanna asked.

Sarah answered, "No, I would just like your company."

Hanna went into the kitchen to make hot chocolate while Sarah nervously dialed her home number. She heard the normal sound of the phone being answered, then, "Is that you, Sarah?" Not the usual "Hello."

"It is I, Sarah," was all that she could say.

She listened while she was asked why she hadn't called before, was she all right, did she actually say "It is I, Sarah," and what kind of talk was that?

"If it is all right I will answer all your questions when I get home." Sarah answered. "Please, I need to ask you for something that is very important."

Before she could say more, her father interrupted her, saying, "If it is about the girl Hanna, we have made arrangements for her to come home with you. She will attend school here this year. If all goes well she may stay with us longer. We will talk more when you come home. Now you get to bed."

Together Sarah and Hanna sat on the front porch drinking their hot chocolate. Sarah had to ask, "When did you know you would be coming home with me?"

Hanna answered, "It is not something you know, or not something someone tells you—it is something you are just aware of. I have been waiting for someone to come for me. I am thankful it is you."

Sarah took a deep breath and quietly said, "I have come for you, little cousin."

Way into the night Sarah lay in her bed thinking about the journal and how her life had changed. It was odd listening to her father speak to her in a familiar way that somehow now seemed so different; he was speaking to the little girl he knew and not the girl she had become.

Sarah closed her eyes, letting her mind become free to wander; she recalled how in the journal her great-grandfather's life, like hers, had changed during one summer as well. And what of his sister Ida Belle, who in some ways lived in two worlds: the everyday, visible world and the shadowiness of an invisible world? *Maybe_we all venture into that mysterious world unaware of it.*

Was there an invisible world? She did believe in angels; where did they exist? Her grandfather talked of their ancestors, the children of the middle waters, believing in such an invisible world, although her great-grandfather did not believe in such things—or did he? If only the journal had kept going. She wanted to know more about her great-grandfather.

Her thoughts turned to caverns. She should tell someone about them; who could she tell? What about the one called Quinton? Yes, he would be the one if she could find him. Tomorrow she would have Hanna take her to him.

When Sarah came down to breakfast the next morning, plans were being made for a farewell get-together that afternoon. This morning would be her last chance to ride Misty, to see the caverns and tell Quinton about them. She found Misty and another horse with new blanket saddles when she came to the stables.

She was not surprised this time when Hanna suddenly appeared, saying, "Quinton will already be at the caverns. He is waiting for us." Sarah shook her head, thinking, I did not have to tell Quinton about the caverns had I not seen the dog at the caverns before.

Quinton was at the entrance of the passageway when Sarah and Hanna arrived. "I have found what I have been looking for," he excitedly announced. "It is the oldest cavern. Come with me, I will show you."

Sarah questioningly looked at Hanna as if to say, *Is he all right?* She did not need an answer; Hanna's expression could not be mistaken. Together they followed Quinton into the oldest cavern. He had not stopped talking about sacred knowledge and the men of mystery.

"Please." Sarah sighed. "What are you talking about?"

Hanna asked, "Are you talking about the seven degrees of learning that had to be studied to become one of the holy men, the men of mystery?"

"Well, not exactly," Quinton answered. "More like scenes that can communicate or suggest the sacred knowledge of the seven degrees of learning. Don't ask me how I know just now; I just know."

"This knowledge, why is it important?" Sarah had to ask. "The scenes must have been painted a long time ago; I understand you believe it is sacred knowledge and you are an anthropologist."

"I suppose it is who we are," Quinton said. "I will be here next summer; I hope you both will come back."

Sarah had mixed emotions when her grandfather told her he was only going back with her to sell his studio and move his things to the ranch. She would not tell him she believed it was his grandfather who wrote the journal, inspired him through her to draw the prints of the Native American life, and came to him that night with the images of his ancestors.

What about herself—was she a descendent of the children of the middle waters? She could no longer believe the awareness she experienced or the unusual inspirations that came to her were just because she was just more perceptive than others.

There may be or they may not be an invisible world, Sarah thought. This visible world I thought I knew is shadowy enough for me.

LaVergne, TN USA
05 November 2009
163104LV00002B/4/P